NICE 'N SLEAZY

S.J. LEWIS

The right of S.J. Lewis to be identified as the author of this work as been asserted by them under the *Copyright Amendment (Moral Rights) Action 2000*

This work is copyrighted. All rights are reserved. No part of this book may be reproduced, scanned, copied, stored in a retrieval system, transmitted or recorded, in any form or by any means without the prior written permission of the writer.

All characters and events in this book are entirely fictional. Any resemblance to real persons is purely coincidental. This book is a work of fiction and should be read as such.

Copyright © 2014 S.J. LEWIS

Cover photo © 2014 Stan Merta

Cover layout and design © 2014 Stan Merta

All rights reserved.

ISBN-13: 978-1495988752

ISBN-10: 1495988759

FOR CERI – You are my sun, my moon, my stars...

"Nice 'n Sleazy does it..."

A BLACKROCK PUBLICATION

CHAPTER ONE

As I disembarked from the aeroplane and stepped into the stark brightness and caressing warmth of the sun I instinctively knew I'd made the right decision. My research had been long and arduous. I mean it was a big step deciding to move to a place you've never even visited. Fuerteventura, a new country, new beginnings, an old cliché I know, but that didn't detract from the fact that I was feeling better about myself right now than I'd felt for most of the previous year. The opportunities that presented themselves here would be unlimited. I now had a chance to re-invent myself. Here I could be whatever I wanted to be, me, no-one else calling the shots, ruling my life, forever taking and never giving. Here I could be queen; here in this land where nobody knew me it was I alone who ruled my destiny.

The biggest surprise was that it hadn't been as difficult as I'd expected it to be, leaving behind my old life; my friends, Sam - my German Shepherd I'd had since I was twenty one, my home and most of all my two beautiful daughters.

Lightly the breeze fluttered around my skirt as I caught my first glimpse of the sea, blue and vast to the left, the mountains on my right, red and brown peppered with blackened shadows from the fluffy white cotton wool clouds drifting silently across the endless blue sky. I breathed in the fresh salt tinged air, my first taste of the cool Atlantic then, shifting the strap of my laptop bag I readjusted my blouse, my passport at the ready.

The apartment wasn't as pretty as it had looked on the internet but it was clean and the little balcony leading off from the lounge bathed in the glorious sun for most of the day.

Since I'd made the decision to move over here around two months ago I'd started exercising and following a strict diet, I was virtually a vegetarian nowadays. The good thing was all of my hard work had paid off, I was back to a size twelve and even my inner thighs had stopped chafing like they used to. I knew I looked good, now all I needed was a suntan, oh yes and internet, some things I was prepared to sacrifice but internet, well that was my communication lifeline.

CHAPTER TWO

As the doorbell rang I extinguished my cigarette and peered over the balcony wall.

"Si," I called out in my best Spanish.

"Hi I'm from the internet company," answered a tall dark man in accented English.

"I'll be right down," I replied pulling the lightweight beach shirt over my lotioned and slightly sweaty body, carefully removing my bikini bottoms from between my bum cheeks.

"Hello I'm Antonio." He smiled, his eyes the colour of dark chocolate, discreetly giving me the once over, his teeth white and straight.

"I'm Vanessa," I said offering him my hand. Taking my hand in his he gently pulled me toward him and proceeded to kiss me on the cheek, first on the left and then on the right.

Taken aback I pulled away; I wasn't used to men being

so forward.

"Sorry Vanessa, I didn't mean to offend you, this is how we greet in Spain," he said looking embarrassed.

"It's okay Antonio, I just wasn't expecting it that's all, everyday I learn something new living here and today I've learnt how to say hello the Spanish way," I said not wanting to scare him off before he'd even installed my internet.

"Maybe I can be your Spanish teacher," he replied suddenly cheekily confident.

You had to admire this good looking stranger's brashness but I played ignorant and smiled at him, complementing him on his English.

"I went to English school for one year in Ireland to, how you say, learn. I come from Italy."

"So what made you come to Fuerteventura?" I asked, romantic visions of Antonio punting his way down one of the canals in Venice, Pavarotti warbling in the background as he steered his way through the maze of tourist laden boats whilst they looked on enviously at us as we made our way to our little love nest with its flower laden balcony inches above the water.

"The same reason as everybody else," he replied, "the sun, the beach and also the business opportunities, the island is still growing and you can make a lot of money here if you are clever."

"I'll bear that in mind," I said mildly disappointed. I was hoping everybody that I met here would be artists, musicians, writers, poets; I wasn't expecting to meet enterprising businessmen even if they were this good looking.

After hooking up my internet Antonio left me a card with his number just in case I had any problems and needed his help with anything. Kissing me on both cheeks yet again he promised to come over to see how I was getting on sometime next week. I began counting down the days to when I would see him again from the moment he left.

CHAPTER THREE

So what qualities do you think you could bring to the job?" asked Sandra, the restaurant owner's wife.

For Christ's sake, it's only a waitressing job, I thought studying Sandra's premature wrinkled features, the black bags below her eyes perceptible even behind her large, unflattering, filthy glasses.

A bit of glamour perhaps?

It wasn't as though I needed a job but after two weeks on the island I found I was having difficulty meeting people, everyone I met seemed to be tourists. I suppose it was to be expected, after all Caleta De Fuste was a purpose built tourist town. It was also really small with only about three thousand local residents. Perhaps by entering the employment market I would finally find some friends with similar interests to mine.

After several minutes of me spouting the type of

nonsense that I could tell she wanted to hear I knew that the job had my name on it.

"Can you start tomorrow night?"

"Sure," I replied thinking how lucky I was, the restaurant was only about a hundred metres from my front door. Picking up a bottle of dry white wine on my way home I was almost skipping by the time I entered the apartment block. Things seemed to be looking up. I'd begun drafting notes for my novel just last night, my internet had been functioning far better than I'd been told it would, I'd just secured my first job on the island and lo and behold, Antonio was stood patiently at my door smoking a cigarette.

Could life get any better than this?

"Hola *guapa*," greeted Antonio flashing his wicked smile. "I was going to ask if you want to go for a coffee but I can see we're having wine at your house instead."

"I'm celebrating tonight, I just got a job," I said feeling really pleased with myself yet slightly apprehensive, the gleam in Antonio's eye making me nervously realise that his intentions weren't exactly honourable. I tried to hide my nervousness but I knew it wouldn't be easy. I hadn't been with another man since I'd married nearly twenty one years ago.

Moving inside I poured us both a glass of wine.

"Perhaps we should sit out on the balcony in the sun," I suggested surveying my dismally small and cluttered lounge, my notes for my novel scattered randomly around my desk, all of my innermost thoughts exposed in black and white for the world to see.

"Sure," replied Antonio smiling, "Whatever you like."

We sat sipping at our wine slowly getting to know each other as the sun bloated tourists staggered along the uneven pavement below, a multitude of languages floating up to greet us musically.

Leaning forward Antonio lowered his hand to my knee.

"You want some more wine?" he asked.

I looked deep into his eyes and realised that for the first time since my husband had left me I wanted more than another glass of wine.

Smiling shyly at my uncharacteristic thoughts I nodded at him wordlessly. Getting up Antonio dropped a light casual-like kiss on my lips. I felt the thrill of the promise that the kiss symbolised right down to the butterflies in my belly and the tingling between my thighs.

"Perhaps we drink inside," he suggested, his hand lightly brushing against my breast as he led me inside. I felt myself shiver involuntary.

Sitting side by side on the cheap couch, Antonio leaned over and gently tilting my head towards him he kissed me full on my mouth, his tongue softly but insistently forcing my lips apart as he probed my mouth, his hand masterfully sliding up the inside of my thigh, gently brushing at the crotch of my panties before moving back down along my thigh, his touch feather-light and electric.

I sighed, our tongues still twisting and I could feel my breathing getting heavier as I slid further down the couch. I parted my legs, wanting more than ever to fell his touch as his hand returned to my crotch gently rubbing me through the sheer fabric, my insides suddenly hot and heavy. Pulling back he looked into my eyes and eased his fingers under the elastic of my panties, his fingers rubbing gently at my aching flesh, slowly at first and then with more insistence. I could feel the momentum building and as he slipped his fingers deep inside me I climaxed so quickly I was almost embarrassed. As I opened my eyes Antonio smiled at me wickedly and kissed me hard on my mouth.

Reaching down I unbuttoned Antonio's shorts where they pooled at his feet. Grasping his hardened cock with both my hands I pulled him towards me and ran my tongue over the glistening end of his shaft. He pushed me away and dropping to his knees he pulled my panties to one side and entered me with a grunt, his cock, far longer than I was used to, pushing hard against my cervix. It had been so long since I'd had a man and I heard myself groaning with pleasure as he ground into me, his hurried thrusts bringing us both to a shuddering climax very quickly.

We collapsed into each other's arms and Antonio smiled and kissed me gently.

"Now it is time for us to have coffee. I am Italian. The only time I have coffee is when I wake up and after I fuck."

I watched in a daze as he stepped over his shorts and made his way over to the kitchen.

I've got a butt-naked Italian stud in my kitchen, I thought happily as I waited for my coffee and hopefully for round two of what I anticipated was going to be a long night.

CHAPTER FOUR

I decided to wait another month until I moved in with Antonio.

Despite the age gap we were getting on famously and he wasn't like any other person of his age that I'd met. Almost every night after work Antonio would be waiting outside for me and we would walk along the dark and breezy pathway on the seafront, the waves crashing against the rocks, the sea spray cool and salty, eventually stopping at the illuminated harbour to watch the fish twisting and turning, their silvery flecks like exploded flashbulbs in the clear water.

My eldest daughter Natalie was coming over for a fortnight in a week's time and it wouldn't have been right to impose her on Antonio for a full two weeks. As much as I loved her she could be a moody cow at the best of times and she still hadn't really got over Jeff and I being divorced. I also got the feeling that she harboured an underlying sense of abandonment since I'd decided to move to Fuerteventura and left her to live with her dad. I would have to work on that once she came over.

In the meantime I'd bought myself a little ex-rental hatchback. It was only three years old but it had galactic mileage on its clock and the scars and dents of a severely uncared for vehicle but it was a car and it was cheap. My divorce settlement money and the inheritance from the death of my dad wouldn't stretch as far as the two-seater convertible I'd rather have had.

In the four months I'd been here I hadn't really travelled outside of the resort so I planned to take off early one morning and discover the rest of the island before Natalie arrived. At least that way I could show her around knowledgeably. I'd been told it was relatively easy to get about and that the chances of getting lost were slim but always the pessimist I'd packed a blanket, a flask of tea and a couple of sandwiches just in case.

The main roads were terrifying, huge lorries and cement mixes riding inches from my bumper before rattling past with a blast of their horns; my little car rocking on it's skinny wheels as if caught in a hurricane. The roundabouts were worse; it seemed that the only way of negotiating them was by closing your eyes, putting your foot down and simply hoping for the best. Once I got off the main road I began to relax. Here the roads were quiet and straight and I even managed to coax a little bit of speed out of my protesting car.

My relaxation however was short lived as I turned towards the mountain range on the left. Although the road surfaces seemed virtually brand new the tarmac began to narrow rapidly and every new turn introduced yet another blind curve. To top it all off there were sheer drops on both sides and the only thing that stopped cars from going over the mountains edge were these huge white concrete blocks randomly spaced out with gaps big enough to drive straight through and into oblivion. I gripped the steering wheel in panic, my knuckles white, and slowed down to a near walking pace. Luckily there was no one behind me, in fact there didn't seem to be anyone on the roads at all. They'd probably driven on these roads once and vowed never to do them again which was exactly how my mindset was working right now.

Coming up on the right hand side I spotted a lay-by and pulled in. Tears were streaming silently down my face and my hands were shaking so badly I could barely pick up my mobile phone. Shielding the screen from the sun streaming through my windscreen the No Signal message scrolled back at me mockingly. I began to cry harder.

CHAPTER FIVE

When I awoke the next morning next to a naked Roger I tried to work out if it was guilt or exhilaration that I felt. Roger had been my saviour, my knight in shining armour and if he hadn't pulled over to make sure that I was okay I think I would still be sitting shivering in the lay-by on top of the mountains. His friend Hans had driven Roger's car and Roger had driven mine back to his sprawling villa in the south of the island. I'd sat in the passenger seat, eyes screwed shut until we reached the end of the mountain range.

His offer of spending the rest of the day besides his pool drinking fine white wine from his underground wine cellar had proved far too tempting to refuse and before long I realised that I'd drunk far too much wine to consider driving home and so the inevitable had happened. I'd felt a slight tug of guilt as Roger had led me to his bedroom, *was I turning into a slut?* but the sex was so mind-blowingly delicious that I found myself doing things I'd never even thought possible. Strangely enough I didn't feel embarrassed or uncomfortable afterwards about what we'd done so I took this as a positive sign that there was a new Vanessa lurking somewhere beneath the old exterior.

Was I cheating on Antonio?

I wasn't sure that I was, it wasn't like we'd made a commitment of exclusivity to each other, and for all I know he could be sleeping with half of the town behind my back. I shifted in the bed and felt the familiar ache that accompanied me after a big work out session in the gym ripple through my stomach muscles and my thighs.

I've been well and truly Rogered, I thought happily as Roger stirred next to me, his unrelenting erection tenting the duvet above him.

CHAPTER SIX

"I'm thirty seven years old Antonio, you're only twenty five; you should be seeing girls your own age."

"But I don't want girls my own age I want you; I have only wanted you since the day we met."

Things were not going well between the two of us but this was our first full blown argument since we'd got together. It hadn't helped that my daughter Natalie had hated Antonio from the moment she laid eyes on him. Although she only spent a couple of days with him she made it blindingly obvious how she felt and she would go out of her way to make his life miserable. I felt bad for thinking the way I did but secretly I was glad that she was only over for two weeks. She could be a real pain in the arse. In the fortnight that Natalie spent with me I'd only seen Antonio about once a week and the fact that we'd gone without having sex the entire time had not only frustrated me but I could tell that Antonio was furious about not only the lack of sex but with the lack of respect that Natalie showed him at any available moment.

"You can't let your daughter control your life like that. She comes here on holiday, destroys our life, and then simply fucks off back to England."

The truth was our time spent more or less apart from each other had taken the shine off of our relationship and I wasn't sure that it would ever be the same again. I began to notice the little flaws that I'd been oblivious to before, little things that I shouldn't really let bother me started to irritate me. Stuff that we would normally discuss or simply accept suddenly became important, like how he would crack his fingers when he was nervous or how he would always light a cigarette just as we were about to do something.

It's funny how time apart can do that to you!

He was also starting to whine now and if it's one thing that I hate then it's a whining man. Jeff my ex husband was a whiner and look where his whining got him, stuck with that fat Polish bitch in a loveless relationship.

"Listen Antonio it's final. I'm not moving in with you and I think you should leave now. Come back tomorrow and pick up your stuff, I think it's better that we're not together anymore."

I cried into my pillow that night, not for what was but for what might have been. Antonio was a good man, well boy really, and the few months we'd had together had been good but it was never meant to last. The age gap, the cultural differences and the fact that Roger had shown me how sex could really be with the right person had signalled to me that the time had come for us both to move on was what I was telling myself.

Was Roger the right person?

Probably not although I didn't know him well enough to make that assumption, but the sex, well that was exactly the type of thing that I was looking for.

By morning I was ready for my next challenge. I needed to get on with my book which I'd neglected since Natalie had arrived and I needed to find somewhere else to live since I'd already handed my notice in on my apartment in anticipation of moving in with Antonio. Perhaps it was time to look for a new job too. They say a change is as good as a holiday, and boy was I ready for a holiday.

.

CHAPTER SEVEN

I popped into Shirley's hairdressers and impulsively decided to have my hair cut short. I loved the new me, the old me would never have considered doing anything so drastic and spontaneous. Once Shirley had finished I decided to go blonde. After three hours at the salon I was unrecognisable.

Sandra had been surprisingly amicable about me leaving the restaurant and had even paid me out my entire holiday pay without me having to beg for it, so I had no concern about having to dig into my savings to keep myself going whilst I looked for an apartment and a job. I pondered on the idea of moving to another town. Living in such a small place everybody seemed to know your business and it would be nice to move somewhere busier where I could reclaim my anonymity. Without giving it too much thought I packed my meagre belongings into my car and made the short move up to the north of the island.

CHAPTER EIGHT

The advantage of having a car was that you could live on the outskirts of town for a much cheaper rent as the properties were in less demand. I chose a pretty little two bedroom bungalow on the outskirts of the sand dunes about three kilometres from the centre of Corralejo. The small garden consisted of crushed volcanic stone with a few scraggy cacti and several piles of dry dog shit left by the previous owner, well the owner's dog, hopefully not the owner!

There was a small garden centre not far from the house so I purchased a few inexpensive and strange looking plants and set about picking up shit and planting my newly acquired flora. Converting the second bedroom into an office, I stuck up a large cork-board to attach my Post-It notes to. I'm a sucker for Post-It notes and will find any reason to scribble on those little yellow bits of paper. As my book began to progress I would write out each of the characters namesd and characteristics and attach them to the cork-board where they would flutter like trapped butterflies in the gentle breeze that wafted its way inland from the Atlantic.

The contrast between Corralejo and Caleta De Fuste was immediate. When I was doing my research I found my initial attraction to Caleta was the supposed quietness, the couples or family friendly nature of the place and the lack of nightclubs and lager louts. The reality of this once you'd settled here quickly wore off when you realised that the smaller the place the bigger the gossip. The lack of things to do created a cultural vacuum in which everybody and anybody discussing other people's business with reckless abandon seemed to be the only form of entertainment. I soon figured out that it was the type of place where if you passed wind in public then by the end of the day you had dropped a large and smelly load in your pants.

Corralejo on the other hand was big and sprawling and suited to either a quiet or hedonistic lifestyle. Here nobody judged you and you were pretty much left to your own devices. Although an ugly town the beaches on the outskirts were some of the best in the world. Huge powdery white sandy dunes stretched out as far as the eye could see and the ocean was a permanently sparkling turquoise. As the summer temperatures began to rise I took to driving over to the quiet part of the beach within the dunes to take a late afternoon swim. Usually there was no one around besides the occasional dedicated nudist. I admit I was shocked when I first saw them parading around with everything on show but before long I got used to it and sort of enjoyed the sheer quirkiness of it. I thought about my friends in the UK who would be huddled up indoors next to the fire whilst I was sitting on a pure white beach watching a naked man or woman parade about as if it were perfectly normal to be butt naked in public and reflected on how lucky I was to have this on my doorstep. I envied the ease in which the nudists carried themselves along the sand and I vowed that I would try it myself one day when no one was around.

After four weeks of job hunting I was finally called back for a second interview at a large estate agency. The pay was almost non-existent but they offered a reasonable commission for any successful sales and the fact that the office was air conditioned sold it to me.

I accepted the position. It had to be better than waitressing.

Once I'd started working I settled into a steady routine. Up and out of bed at six, at the gym from six thirty to seven fifteen, home at seven thirty, shower, eat and get dressed by eight fifteen, write until nine fifteen and at work by nine thirty. Work until three, home by three fifteen, changed and ready for the beach by three thirty, arrive at the beach by three forty five, swim until four fifteen, or four thirty if I was feeling self indulgent, then back home by at least five. Shower and then prepare dinner and relax. I loved my routine and stuck to it for six days a week. On Sunday I rested like all Goddesses should.

CHAPTER NINE

"Come on Vanessa, it'll be fun," insisted Susan, the other sales representative that worked at our office. "When last did you go out for a drink anyway?"

I shook my head and ashamedly admitted that I hadn't been out for a drink since moving up here. I knew I sounded lame but I was happy with my life and my routine and I couldn't imagine anything worse than sitting in a sweaty bar watching your workmates get drunk.

"You might meet your prince charming," added Susan.

"With my luck he'll just turn back into a frog once I get to know him," I replied.

Susan knew that I was writing a book about a girl trying and failing to find her prince charming and she firmly believed that I was basing it on my own real life experience. I was beginning to wonder if perhaps she was right.

"Well at least you might find someone to scratch that itch," she said pointing at my crotch crudely.

"I've got a set of double A batteries that does that for me," I said grinning. "But hey, you've convinced me. We'll meet up at eight outside the office."

"Cool," said Susan beaming happily, "I bet there's a real wicked streak hidden inside that cool sophisticated façade." She stepped forward and hugged me fiercely. "Really Vanessa, don't look so concerned, we're going to have a great time."

I drove home in silent trepidation. It had been so long since I'd attended any social gatherings, let alone put myself out there amongst the vultures that preyed on this town. Although I loved living here the people that called this island their home were not the type of people I would have chosen to spend time with, and back in England I would have definitely moved in completely different social circles. I should really have savoured the variety rather than shunned it but although I appeared outwardly confident, inside I was a wreck and I'd found the easiest way to avoid being discovered as weak and pathetic was to simply avoid as many social situations as possible. The only trouble with doing this was that sooner or later you had to play along even if it was just to maintain a sort of friendship.

CHAPTER TEN

I pulled on my little black dress and studied myself in the mirror.

Not bad really!

My panty lines were plainly visible under the sheer fabric and with a quick sense of bravado I pulled up the hem of the dress and removed them. Since I'd finally succumb to the lure of nudism on what I considered my own private stretch of beach I'd found a confidence in my body that I'd never had before. Checking my make-up once more, making sure my crow's feet were carefully hidden, I snatched up my bag, stepping over my discarded panties hurriedly before I changed my mind about the underwear.

Waiting for Susan outside of the office I couldn't help but feeling like one of those street hookers in my short dress. I consciously tried to avoid all eye contact but I could actually feel the men who passed me by looking me up and down even if I didn't see them doing it. I felt violated and uncomfortable and it was with a sense of relief I spotted Susan heading towards me.

"Wow, you look hot," she said touching my arm and pulling back as if burned.

"You don't look too bad yourself, it's amazing what a bit of make-up can do," I said laughing.

"Why you cheeky cow!"

Susan punched me lightly on my shoulder as we click-clacked along the pavement in our heels, pushing our way through sweaty tourists towards an unspoken destination. I followed like a lamb to the slaughter.

Susan went to get the drinks in and I was left standing next to one of those circular tables attached to a pole that you tend to find in those dismally cheap bars. The over-bright interior looked really tacky with all its flashing neon lights advertising weak lager and the pseudo Americanisms should have been laughable but instead they were just sad. The crowd seemed to be a happy mix of tanned locals and sunburnt tourists. I gazed over to the bar where the pimple faced barman juggled drinks like a wannabe Tom Cruise circa nineteen eighty something and realised that this was going to be a long night. The only things I had in common with Susan were that we worked in the same place and we were the same sex. Other than that we were poles apart.

I'd never been much of a drinker and because I'd had Natalie so young Jeff and I hadn't really gone out much. In many ways Antonio and I were well suited as, like most Italians, he wasn't really a drinker or much of a socialite and we had spent most of our time either at each other's homes or taking an evening stroll on the beach. I realised I missed those simple times but I knew that it would have been selfish to have stayed with him. The age difference was huge and whilst not a problem for possibly a few years, before long Antonio would have been eyeing up younger women and looking at me like I was his mother and by then I would be old and left alone....

"Vanessa! Vanessa, gee girl you were miles away then. Drinks are here." Susan plonked our drinks on the flimsy table along with two small glasses of vicious looking blue liquid.

"Complementary shots," she said by way of explanation, picking up one of the small glasses and handing it to me.

"What are they?" I asked.

"Who cares, it's alcohol, just down it and be grateful it's free"

She raised her glass and touching our glasses together with a clink, I dubiously downed the vile tasting substance.

"Urgh!" I breathed out what felt like the fire of Hades. "I don't ever want another of those in my life," I said taking a large gulp on my vodka and lime in the hope of washing away the taste.

"You get one free with every drink," said Susan.

"I can see why they give them away. You're welcome to mine when we get the next round."

"Actually I think I'll give them a miss too. I reckon they give them away in the hope that you'll get pissed quickly and not notice how much they charge for drinks in this place. Five euros each those were."

Neither of us were short of cash, sales had been good

over the last few months but there was talk of an upcoming recession that was supposed to start in America and spread worldwide in the near future and already some of the property developers and banks were beginning to show signs of nervousness. Having lived through two fairly big recessions in the UK in my lifetime I listened carefully to the business news, my nest egg wasn't big enough to squander unnecessarily.

I tried to be enthusiastic about the bar I found myself in but I just couldn't be. My vodka tasted as cheap as the overpowering cologne the local pick up artists seemed to be wearing and the music was just awful, some misogynistic R&B hip-hop trash that only white boys under the age of eleven would appreciate. I so wanted this night to turn out good but I knew as long as we hung around here it would be a disaster. I downed my vodka and caught Susan's eye.

"Let's get out of here. I want to dance." I demanded.

Susan didn't need much persuading.

"Sorry I brought you to that dive," said Susan as we clomped our way along the pavement. "It didn't used to be like that, believe it or not that used to be the place to be seen. It must have new owners or something."

I breathed in the fresh air, grateful to be outside.

By now all the bar touts had appeared on the pavements, their jovial invitations and the conflicting music pulsating from the different bars fighting for our attention as we headed down the high street towards the beach. I hadn't danced since my best friend Michelle's wedding, which must have been a good four or five years ago. I was looking forward to dancing again.

CHAPTER ELEVEN

I slumped against the vinyl backed chair in the darkened booth. My sweat soaked dress was clinging to me like a second skin. My feet ached but it was a good ache. Perhaps I would have blisters tomorrow. The Reflex Club was just what I needed. All the familiar 80′s dance tunes that we could sing along to whilst we strutted our stuff without a care in the world. I loosened off my shoes and tucked my feet underneath me.

Susan grinned at me slyly. "I never knew you were such an exhibitionist."

"I'm not an exhibitionist, I'm only dancing."

"I'm not talking about your dancing," She pushed her hair back from out of her eyes, "You're not wearing any knickers."

I could feel myself blush. "Oh my God; how do you know that?" I asked.

"Those under floor lights," she said laughing. "They

make your dress totally see through."

"And you only thought of telling me this now."

"Well, you were enjoying yourself and I didn't want to spoil it for you, besides, you're famous now. Didn't you see all those guys snapping photos of you on their camera phones?"

"Susan you're such a bitch, you could have at least told me earlier."

"Aw, relax. All you've done is create a fantasy for those guys to have a wank over when they get back to their lonely, pathetic, man-cave bachelor pads. You've enjoyed tonight, I can tell, and that's the most important thing."

"I hope I don't bump into any of the guys here tonight at work on Monday, that'll be so embarrassing."

"Why, have you taken to not wearing knickers to work either?" asked Susan laughing.

"Fuck off, don't be ridiculous. God my feet hurt."

"Yeah mine too but hey, I love this song. I'm going for one more dance before we call it a night...You coming?"

"Yeah right, like I'm going to dance around butt naked by choice in front of these losers. I'll give it a miss thank you."

I watched as Susan shook her ass to Billy Idol's growl. I had indeed enjoyed tonight. Perhaps The Reflex could become part of my social calendar even if I had committed the *faux pas* of revealing a little bit too much of myself to its patrons, at least the guys here weren't hanging around me like I was a bitch on heat.

Suddenly someone slid into the booth on the opposite side of the table, someone tall, dark, handsome and Italian.

"Vanessa. Is that you?"

CHAPTER TWELVE

I'd avoided seeing Antonio since the day we'd parted and after the first week I even found it in myself to remove his number from my phone.

He flashed his wicked grin at me, the same grin he'd given me the first time we'd had sex in my little apartment in Caleta.

"I knew it was you. Wow it's so good to see you. You look great. I thought you'd left the island or something."

"Hey Antonio," I smiled back at him, surprisingly pleased to see him. "What brings you here to the evil depths of Corralejo?"

"My cousin is over from Italy and she fancied a night out. You know this isn't my type of thing. What are you doing here anyway?"

"I moved up here after we split." I noticed Antonio flinch as the word split came out of my mouth. "I live here now." I leaned across the table in order to be heard.

"What have we here?" asked Susan sliding beside me in the booth. "I turn my back for five minutes and you go and find yourself a man."

"Susan this is an old friend, Antonio. Antonio – Susan, Susan – Antonio."

They nodded their heads in greeting.

"Listen Vanessa, I'm going to get a cab home, I'm bushed…I'll leave you guys to catch up," she added with a twinkle in her eye. "I'll see you at work on Monday. It was nice meeting you Antonio."

With that Susan left the two of us looking into each other's eyes, the cheesy eighties soundtrack washing over us like a bad John Hughes film.

CHAPTER THIRTEEN

The cab ride back to my place felt strangely familiar with Antonio at my side. It was weird how I'd only been thinking about him earlier this very night and now here he was right next to me. His cousin had returned to her hotel and after we'd dropped her off Antonio had insisted that he made sure that I got home safely. I presumed that this was just a ploy on his behalf but I was happy to go along with it.

Antonio was looking good; in fact he was looking better than when we were together. Time apart suited him. In the flashing sodium lamp light reflecting through the taxi window he looked more rugged, more manly, and it was obvious that he'd been working out in the gym, his dark arms muscular and taut.

We'd make a great looking couple, I thought ironically.

I recalled kissing those full lips, those strong arms around me as we made love and tried to push the thoughts from my mind. The taxi driver was saying something but I wasn't listening, locked in my own private fantasy.

"¿Aqui señora?"

"Si, gracias," I replied, snapping out of my daydream, realising we'd already reached my house.

Antonio paid the cab driver and we stepped out into the cool night air.

"Is it okay if I come in?" asked Antonio. "Just to talk," he added.

"Sure," I answered waving the taxi off. I felt a nervous excitement in my stomach, not unlike the first time that Antonio and I had made love.

We sat and spoke for several hours and by four a.m. I could feel my eyelids getting droopy. I was waiting for Antonio to make a move on me so that I could let him down gently but true to his word he seemed solely intent on talking.

"I'm going to bed, I'm really tired," I said expecting him to follow but instead he stood up kissed me on both cheeks as was his way, and said goodbye. I watched as the door lock clicked behind him and could hear him calling a cab through the flimsy door.

I felt a mix of emotions as I hit the pillow.

Was it possible to feel both horny and exhausted at the same time?

I slept, dreaming of Antonio boldly going where he'd never been before, only waking at nearly ten a.m. Still half asleep I reached into my side drawer and removed my Rabbit I'd bought online a month after splitting from Antonio and brought myself awake with the vibrator's gentle buzzing and a much needed orgasm.

CHAPTER FOURTEEN

"Sooo..., tell me all about it," insisted Susan the moment I stepped into the office on the Monday morning.

Susan's own love life was so complicated that anything you told her would pale in comparison. A year ago she used to work for a rival estate agency here in Corralejo and at the time Susan and her husband were not getting along. She started an affair with her boss who was a sweet single Indian man who'd never had a proper girlfriend. The affair didn't really go anywhere and from what I could work out she had mainly used him as a shoulder to cry on. They shared a few fumbling kisses a couple times in the back of the office but it hadn't gone much further than that. Her husband was convinced that she was having an affair with her boss so to appease him she left the rival agency and started work here.

Her move hadn't helped their relationship and rather than forgetting about her old boss, whenever she began arguing with her husband she would end up phoning him up at all hours to complain about her husband. Her old boss was still smitten with her so she would take advantage of this, constantly using him as her back up when things went wrong, again only as a shoulder to cry on. It was obvious that she was simply hedging her bets should her marriage fall apart for good and some days when I would see her together with her ex boss in the café down the road from the office, I would have to force myself not to march in and tell the poor sap that he should stop playing second fiddle and that he should go out and find himself a proper girlfriend.

Still, it was better to not get involved.

"Nothing happened Susan. Antonio and I are just friends."

"Come on Vanessa, I saw that look in your eye. I know what that look means."

"Okay look, you want the truth. Antonio and I were together back when I lived in Caleta. We had a thing but it's over, has been for a long time. I haven't even got his number." I said throwing her my phone. "Look for yourself."

I could see the disappointment in her face as she scrolled through my small list of contacts.

"Shit girl, he was hot...You're serious, you didn't even do it for old times' sake?"

"Not even for old times´ sake. All we did was talk."

"So how are your feet?"

"Still sore to be honest but I enjoyed myself. Your hubby still okay about you going out on a girl's night out?"

"Not really. He thinks I was out with Sanjay again but he

hasn't actually said that. I tell you if it wasn't for Hannah I'd be long gone."

Hannah was Susan's two year old daughter and the semi-permanent glue that somehow kept her marriage together. It seemed to me that most mothers in bad relationships tended to make the same mistake of staying with their partners for their children's sake, not realising that they are simply dragging out the inevitable and making their children's life miserable to boot.

Having gone through the same experience I felt qualified to feel this way but I was wise enough not to share my thoughts. In my experience the moment you became involved was the moment everything backfired on you.

With age comes wisdom.

That reminded me, I was turning thirty eight in a couple of weeks time.

CHAPTER FIFTEEN

The week passed by insignificantly until the Friday when I arrived at work. Susan and my boss were waiting for me besides my desk. You could tell that they had just shared a private joke as both of their eyes were twinkling with amusement.

"Okay guys; come on, what's going on, what's so funny?" I asked.

My boss managed to mumble the word nothing before they both burst into fits of laughter. I followed their eyes to a blank A5 piece of paper sitting conspicuously on my desk. Quickly I snatched it up as they broke down into even more laughter.

I turned the paper over and looked at it in horror. Susan stepped forward striking a silly pose and began to guffaw. Tears of laughter ran down her face.

It was a flyer for The Reflex, the club we'd been at last week, the centre piece of which was, yes you guessed it, yours truly. Head back, eyes closed, one arm in the air, legs slightly apart and those god-damned under-floor lights shining straight up my dress, I looked almost naked. My boss stood in the same pose as the one on the flyer as Susan doubled up laughing, tears and snot running down her face.

I could feel myself turning puce.

"Where did you get this?" I asked.

"They're everywhere," giggled Susan wiping at her face with a tissue. "Every bar, restaurant, hotel, even the tourist office has a pile of them. I got this from a kid who was handing out flyers last night when I left work. You're famous girl," laughed Susan striking the now familiar pose.

I sulked about the flyer for at least an hour before it was time to meet with some new clients.

"Please don't show it to anyone?" I asked knowing that Susan probably had her bag full of them. "Especially not my clients."

"I won't do that. I promise," said Susan stepping out of her chair and raising her hand, striking what was soon to become known as The Vanessa Pose.

That afternoon I broke from my usual routine and headed over to one of the Spanish salons. My previous short hair had begun to grow long once again and the darker roots were beginning to show. This time I chose a drastically short cut and dyed my hair a deep and dark red. I left the salon confident that I wouldn't be recognised as the girl from The Reflex flyer.

CHAPTER SIXTEEN

When I woke up the following Thursday morning I expected to feel different but I didn't. Thirty eight was a landmark birthday for me as my mother had died before she'd reached this milestone. Both Natalie and my younger daughter Angie had e-mailed me to wish me a good day and although in the big scheme of things this was just another day, to me it felt very special. Even though it had been nearly a week since I'd changed my hairstyle and colouring it still took me by surprise when I caught my reflection in the bathroom mirror and today was no exception. The Spanish hairdressers here didn't really have a great reputation, they were used to working on the coarser Spanish hair, but they had done a great job on me and I felt confident that I could pass for at least eight to ten years younger than I was.

As I worked out in the gym I was surprised how awake I felt this morning. I'd been checking my e-mails last night and before I knew it I had got involved on the computer and sidetracked by my book. When I looked at my watch I'd realised it was two thirty a.m. Late though it was I was still amazed to discover that I'd managed to write an additional two thousand words. My agent would be pleased.

When I got into work that morning both Susan and Bill, my boss broke into an awful rendition of Happy Birthday, mixing the English and Spanish versions together in a terrifying cacophony. I laughed happily at their enthusiasm. My boss, presented me with a small cake, thankfully festooned with only a few candles and Susan disappeared to the back of the office only to return with a huge gaily wrapped present.

"Go on open it," she enthused eagerly.

I assumed from the size and shape of it that it was a painting of some sort. Delicately removing the bow, I tore at the paper and revealed my present.

I feigned embarrassment as I didn't wish to come across as vain but in all honesty what they had given me was probably the best birthday present I'd ever received. The flyer from The Reflex had been professionally blown up to an almost life-size proportion and framed. You could see the euphoria on my face now that the picture was so clear. Placing the picture onto the floor gently upright, I stood back and admired myself before turning to hug the two of them.

"Vanessa you look great," said Bill pointing to their gift.

"Yeah you do," said Susan. "And we can see your Brazilian," she added laughing.

When I got home that night I hung the picture in a pride

of place above the desk where I write. My daughters would be thrilled when they saw it; I mean how many non-celebrity mums end up as a poster girl for what could be considered one of the hottest clubs on the island?

.

CHAPTER SEVENTEEN

Because my birthday was on a school night Susan and I arranged to go out on the Saturday. No prizes for guessing where we were going. I was looking forward to it knowing that there was no chance of anyone recognising me from the flyer in my present guise.

Susan's husband had happily agreed to allow her to go but changed his mind that Thursday night. Another of their arguments had flared up and Susan had driven off in a huff. Because it was a full moon the night sky was almost as bright as daylight and, without any sense of purposeful direction, she had ended up alongside the sand dunes, the moonlight painting their usual stark whiteness with a purple and blue tinge. She pulled over and cried for a while before pulling herself together and phoning Sanjay.

"God, you didn't did you?" I asked incredulously over coffee the following morning.

"Well you know, the dunes looked so romantic bathed

in moonlight and well, one thing led to another and before I knew it..." She shrugged.

"Are you going to tell Mark?"

"Not a chance. He'd probably kill me, and Sanjay as well."

"Not that it's any of my business," I said measuring my words carefully, "but you can't keep going on like this. You have responsibility and you and Mark have to talk about things, not just for the sake of your marriage but for Hannah's sake too."

"I know, I know but my head's all over the place. Sanjay wants me to leave Mark and he's quite happy to accept Hannah as well."

"Well of course he has to accept Hannah, she's part of the package," I said interrupting her.

"Yeah, you know what I mean. You know Mark and I used to have a great relationship but something went wrong along the way. I don't know if it was the move over here or me giving birth but something has changed and I don't think we'll ever get it back."

"Far be it for me to give people advice but don't you think you like the idea of a relationship with Sanjay because it's something new and exciting. New relationships always seem like, I don't know, they seem like you've finally found the one you've been looking for. You know the saying new brooms sweep clean, well it was like that with me and Antonio for a while, you know the guy from the club, but over time people change and unfortunately you have to change too if you want the relationship to continue working. My mother used to say that the flowers of romance are littered with thorns and what I think she was saying was that you have to take the rough with the smooth, not only in your relationships but in life in general. She certainly used to keep my dad on his toes."

"It's easy talking about it with friends but Mark, Mark just clams up the moment we try talking through our problems. It would be so much easier if he would just go out and have an affair so that I'd have a legitimate reason for leaving him."

CHAPTER EIGHTEEN

Saturday night turned into a disaster. Feeling lazy after a busy day with clients I'd ordered a take away curry the night before. By Saturday morning the food had gone straight through me and my stomach kept cramping terribly. We'd arranged to meet outside the office once again and this time before I left I stood in my bedroom with the lights off in front of a mirror flashing a torch between my legs. I knew I must have looked ridiculous but I wanted to make sure that the dress I bought at Zara the week before wasn't going to give the patrons of the club more than what they had paid for.

In the meantime Susan and Mark's fighting had escalated into a full on screaming match before she met up with me and even with her make-up on I could tell she'd been crying again.

"Should we give the club a miss tonight?" I asked. "My stomach isn't feeling too good, I think that take away curry I had last night wasn't too healthy and not being harsh or anything, but you're not looking like you're in the mood to party," I said touching her lightly on her arm.

"Would you mind? I feel really bad but I'm not sure I'll even be able to make it through the night to be honest. I don't know what's wrong with me but I seem to be crying all the time. I hope to God I'm not pregnant. Should we just call into the nearest bar and have a quick one just to celebrate your birthday and to mourn my unhappiness?"

"I don't mind, as long as you don't want to go back to that crap bar we went to last time."

We stepped into a glum English themed pub and ordered drinks which we drank in a similar fashion to the scattering of patrons finding themselves seated haphazardly throughout the establishment; in dutiful glumness.

I was back home by nine fifteen.

Taking an Imodium in an attempt to settle my stomach I curled up on the couch with a draught of my book that I'd printed out earlier. At ten thirty my mobile rang loudly, startling me from the light doze I'd fallen into, causing me to scatter the pile of A4 sheets across the tiled floor as I reached for it. I checked my watch and wondered who could be calling me at this time of night.

"Vanessa, sorry to bother you, can we come over, Hannah and I?" sniffed Susan.

"Sure Susan, are you okay?"

"Yeah I'm fine, I'll explain when I get over."

I picked my novel up from off of the ground and did a quick tidy around. The Imodium seemed to have worked for which my stomach and my burning sphincter were eternally grateful. I wondered what had happened between Susan and Mark. It wasn't like her to leave with Hannah in tow, this time it must be serious.

As Susan's headlights raked a path into my lounge I realised that I needed to set up the camp bed for Hannah. I quickly rushed into my office and pulled out the makeshift bed.

Opening the door I watched as Susan shuffled up the driveway, a sleeping Hannah in her arms. I guided her through into the office and pointed at the camp bed. Susan lay Hannah down carefully as I passed her a blanket. Hannah shifted a little in her sleep and then, grabbing a handful of the blanket and tucking it around herself, she fell back into a deep slumber.

How I envied the sleep of children.

We headed back into the lounge.

"You want something to drink?" I asked. "Tea, coffee, water, beer, wine, fruit juice...whatever?"

"Mark's having an affair," said Susan breaking down into tears. "I caught him fucking her in our bed. Can you believe it? In our bed!"

I tried to conjure up some sort of anger towards Mark but I couldn't really. After all Susan was having an affair with Sanjay. Really their whole marriage was a sham. Pouring us a glass of red wine each I let her ramble on and get it out of her system.

"You don't mind if Hannah and I stay for a while do you?" she asked.

"Sure, no problem, stay as long as you want; you'll either have to share with me or kip on the couch." I answered.

"Thanks Vanessa, I didn't know what else to do. That's it now, I've left him for good now, the bastard, he can fuck right off. That filthy bitch Christine, in our bed, I can't believe the cheek of it."

"Christine, Christine who; not Christine the piss head?"

"The very one; I can't believe it. God, to think I've slept in the same bed as that slag; It doesn't bear thinking about."

Christine the piss head rented an apartment from Susan. Everybody in Corralejo knew who she was. We'd been warned by other agencies not to take her on as a tenant but the irony of it was that Susan had felt sorry for her and had organised an apartment for her, not through the agency but through a private contact that she had. She'd warned her that the landlord didn't take too kindly to tenants that didn't pay their rent and that if she happened to miss a month she stood a chance of getting both of her legs broken and, as far as I knew, she was still walking so perhaps she'd been good on the payments.

"Jeez girl, you'd have to be pretty desperate to want to shag Christine, I'd heard she'd do just about anyone for a bottle of vodka," I said surprised.

"There's a lot I haven't told you Vanessa. Mark and I have only had sex twice in the last six months. There's just nothing there."

"But still Susan... Christine? I mean she's even got a beard," I said shivering at the thought.

"Well he can shag her as much as he likes because that's it now, we're finished. I'm taking Hannah and he can keep the stupid house, it's not worth what we paid for it nowadays anyway. I just want my share of the money in the UK account, there's over fifty grand in there from when we sold our house. Those two can live together and see who can grow the longest beard," she said smiling grimly.

CHAPTER NINETEEN

It was strange going from the solitude of living by yourself to suddenly having your home invaded by other people. Hannah was a little treasure to have around but served as a constant reminder of how grateful I was that my two had grown up. Susan had turned from weepy to lividly angry, especially when she found out that Mark had been shagging Christine behind her back for over a year. I think she was actually more upset that he had managed to get away with it for so long without her finding out and now she felt foolish. She'd phoned Sanjay and told him that she was ready to move in with him and ever since he'd been avoiding her and ignoring her constant phone calls. He had tried to explain to her that he needed to look after his family and that he couldn't move away from home at that moment in time but you didn't need to be a genius to work out that he'd suddenly developed cold feet.

Susan had thankfully chosen the couch rather than

sharing my bed so at least my sleep pattern wasn't interrupted too much but just lately a strange thing seemed to be happening. I would wake up at random times in the evening with a sense that somebody was watching me through my bedroom window. The first couple of times I put it down to the fact that I wasn't used to the house being occupied by others but after the third or fourth time I instinctively knew that I was being spied on. One night I awoke shivering in my bed despite the relative warmth, certain that I could feel prying eyes upon me. Without even thinking about it I leapt out of bed and tore the curtain open catching a quick glimpse of a startled Mark, Susan's husband, before he melted away into the shadows.

My heart was hammering in my chest and I knew that the sudden rush of adrenaline that I'd experienced would not allow me to return to sleep so I headed into the kitchen and poured myself a glass of cold milk. I heard the couch springs creaking and then soft footsteps approaching.

"Hey."

"Hey yourself," said Susan rubbing at the sleep in her eyes. "What are you doing up?" she asked stifling a yawn.

"Your husband woke me up."

Susan paled.

"What? My Mark?"

"Yeah I woke up and found him peeping at me through the window."

"What did he say?"

"Nothing. As soon as he saw me he just legged it but I don't think that it's the first time he's been watching me, I've woken up a couple of times in the last few days and felt as though I was being watched, it's quite scary actually."

"Maybe we should call the police. That should scare him off."

"I don't think it's necessary, besides we've no real proof that he was here."

"I would phone him and warn him off but it'll do no good, I know him well enough to know that's what he wants me to do and I'm not playing into his hands. You've probably scared him off for a while anyway."

I wasn't scared of Mark. I'd always found him smarmy and self righteous at the best of times and he was all but five foot nothing. I swear he used to wear lifters in his shoes when he went out. Next time I'd be ready for him with a baseball bat so he'd better practice a few short sprints before he decides to come back and bother me.

The next morning we went outside to find all four of my tyres slashed. Since Mark had taken their car back we only had my car to ferry Susan and I to work and Hannah to the child minders. I phoned Bill at work and asked if he minded picking us up in the company car and phoned my insurance company as we waited for him to arrive.

I slept fitfully for the next two nights waiting for Mark to return, my mobile phone underneath my pillow in preparation.

On the third night I heard the unmistakable sound of someone shuffling around outside of my window. Carefully I shifted my pillow and speed dialed the local police number that I'd installed onto my phone, whispering my address to the operator on the end of the line.

The police were surprisingly quick and within five

minutes Mark was in custody in the back of the blue and white police vehicle.

Susan and Hannah hadn't even woken up!

When I recounted the events of the night before to Susan the next morning she insisted that it was time for her to move out.

"I didn't want to involve you, you know, I just didn't know who else to turn to but I'm sure between us at the office we can find something suitable for Hannah and I to move into."

I wasn't going to argue with her; I didn't mind having them around but as I'd told her from the very start I didn't want to end up playing piggy in the middle like I was now. Not only did I have to deal with her problematic husband but now Sanjay had taken to calling me asking me hundreds of questions.

Does Susan talk about me?

Do you think Susan loves me?

If I find us a place to stay do you think she'll take me back?

Can I speak to her?

My answers were simple and straightforward. If you want to talk to her then phone her phone not mine and no, she doesn't love you, you yellow bellied loser. Actually I didn't call him that but it didn't stop me from thinking it.

Just as Susan and Hannah moved out I got a phone call from Jeff, my ex. Angie my youngest daughter was coming over to live with me. She'd been given an ultimatum; it was either move over here with me or go into a foster home. It seemed I had no say in the matter.

There's certainly no rest for the wicked in this life.

CHAPTER TWENTY

Angie had always been a difficult and challenging child. Whereas Natalie was well behaved and happy to do whatever you asked her to do, Angie was the complete opposite. I'd always said to Jeff we should have called them Yin and Yang. As soon as she learned to walk Angie challenged any boundaries that she was given. If you took your eye off of her for a second she would disappear only to be found on the other side of a main road having crossed over by herself quite happily. It seemed like she always wanted to get away from not just us, but any person of authority and, to be honest, her anti-establishment stance somehow gained momentum with every new sunrise.

She was a beautiful girl, far prettier than her sister but she would go out of her way to make herself ugly and the facial piercings and homemade tattoos appeared, unapproved, before she'd even turned fourteen. I got the impression she didn't care much for these adornments herself but she knew how much it upset Jeff and I so she continued introducing new ones behind our backs, relishing the arguments that it would cause between us.

She was nearly sixteen now and had just been suspended from her third high school. Teachers gave up on her quickly, not through lack of professionalism but just because it was an impossible task to teach her anything. If she was told something was black she would argue that it was white just for the sake of it, disrupting lessons all the time and causing general mayhem around the school.

I considered myself lucky that she hadn't fallen pregnant yet. Pregnancy was mine and Jeff's biggest fear so we tackled it head on at an early age. We used an improvised reverse psychology, introducing her to almost any boy we laid eyes on hoping that because we approved she wouldn't. This seemed to work really well but I was dreading the day she saw through our anti-pregnancy plan. To be honest though I think most boys were too scared to even think about sleeping with her, her reputation ironically protecting her from even the hardiest of lads.

Although I perhaps portray Angie as a child of Satan himself I loved her with all my heart and would do anything in my power to protect her. She had her moments when she could be the sweet, nice daughter I'd always hoped she would turn out to be but these were so sporadic that they became just a blip on the chart of the general nastiness that followed her around like a bad smell.

She'd been caught doing drugs and drinking in the park on the edge of a rough estate by one of the increasingly rare local police foot patrols and, as soon as the school had

Nice 'n Sleazy

found out, they had suspended her indefinitely. As much as I hated Jeff and his fat Polish bitch of a girlfriend Marta, I couldn't help but feel sorry for them. I knew how much of a handful Angie could be and with no reason to go to school things could only go from bad to worse.

Jeff was hoping that the simple lifestyle over here and the lack of a huge drug culture may thwart Angie's steady decline into the dreaded drug addiction that he always feared. I tried to explain that everybody smoked pot nowadays and that it wasn't a particularly bad thing but he wasn't having it. As far as he was concerned marijuana was but a step away from mainlining heroin. I reckoned Marta played a bit part in his decision but after all they were the ones who had to put up with Angie's shit day in, day out and it was bound to grind them both down eventually.

The biggest concern that I had was the fact that Corralejo, although comparatively tame with regards to some of the burnt out, drug riddled estates that spread across Britain like a bad stain, it still had a reputation for its anything goes attitude and probably wasn't the best of places to try and steer Angie onto the straight and narrow. With this in mind I handed in my notice both on the house and at work and prepared for a move back to the quietness of Caleta De Fuste. I was hoping that my experience in one of the bigger estate agencies in Corralejo would stand me in good stead for a similar position in Caleta.

After three weeks I said a tearful goodbye to Susan and my boss Bill and returned full circle to Caleta, the place where my Fuerteventura experience originated, albeit with a new job and a new home. I promised to drive up every so often to see how the two of them were getting on and I also promised Susan I'd phone her regularly and let her know how things in Caleta were as she was thinking of moving down there herself to get away from Mark. I would miss Corralejo and my relative anonymity but I was heading back to Caleta knowing what to expect and this time I'd chosen a house away from the centre of town, the prying eyes and those endless twitching curtains. My new job was at one of the bigger estate agents and unlike before when I was waitressing, estate agency jobs meant that you weren't always under continuous public scrutiny.

Strangely enough when I turned right up towards Chipmunk Hill and the Traveler's Rest it felt like a sort of homecoming. Perhaps things would work out well this time. As I indicated right at the stop sign halfway up the hill I saw a shirtless Antonio jogging down the hill in a tight pair of shorts. I prayed that he didn't recognise the car but he did and he began frantically waving his arms around like a mad man at me. I pulled over to the side of the road. He leaned into my open window and kissing my cheeks, he flashed his wicked smile.

"You moving back?" he asked indicating all of my stuff piled into the back of the car.

I nodded my head. "Yeah I'm right on the top of the hill."

"I'll help you," he said, and before I even had chance to protest he walked around the front of my car and climbed into the passenger seat.

I could smell his fresh sweat from his recent jog, strangely familiar, and glancing at his naked torso I could feel a jolt between my legs reminding me that it had been a long time since I'd had a man.

This was all I needed, moving house was a difficult enough task, never mind trying to do it whilst I was horny as hell.

As I pulled up outside my new house Antonio began to laugh. It started with a slow chuckle and turned into a full on eye streaming guffaw.

What's so funny?" I asked looking at Antonio as if he was crazy.

"This...This is your new house?" He asked struggling to get the words out between his booming laugh.

"Yes, I don't understand what it is that's so funny."

Antonio reached over and grasped my right hand in his in a firm handshake, his face suddenly serious.

"Welcome to the neighborhood chica, I'm Antonio your new next door neighbor."

CHAPTER TWENTY ONE

After living in a detached house for the last few months it took me a while to get used to being back within a community. The house to the left of mine was incredibly quiet, so much so in fact that I'd often wondered if the tenants had perhaps died within its deathly quiet walls. Antonio on the other hand was remarkably noisy. It didn't bother me too much but it was the intimacies of hearing him having a shit through the walls in the mornings or the late night trickles of his cascading pee that was loud enough to sometimes wake me that made me uncomfortable. If I could hear him, he could hear me and that was where my concern lay.

I contemplating moving house before Angie arrived but I loved the location and the layout of the house, slightly quirky with its two bedrooms, lounge, kitchen and bathroom spread out over three levels, and I would battle to find anything comparable for a similar rent. Plus it was nice in a way having Antonio next door, he'd helped me a lot setting up the house when I first moved in and it was reassuring having a man I knew living beside me. The day Simone moved in was the day my attitude changed.

Okay, I admit jealousy played a huge role in the way I felt and I know that it was unfair for me to expect Antonio to stay single just because I would have preferred it that way, but their lovemaking would keep me awake night after night. Either Antonio's technique had improved or he had learnt to control the trigger far better than he had when he was with me. They would have marathon sessions that would last for anywhere up to two hours at a time and the worst of it was that Simone was a screamer. It wasn't even like there was any build up; she would just start screaming and never stop until it was all over. I slept with my iPod attached to my ears on a nightly basis and I knew that I should actually have a word with them about it but I didn't have the heart. Not only that, but I didn't want to come over as the jealous ex lover that I secretly was.

Now that Christmas was nearly here I began to feel lonely. I always loved Christmas, it was the one time we did everything together as a family regardless of any animosity that we felt towards each other and everything about that time symbolised pure happiness for me; the tree, the decorations, the cards from half forgotten friends, the cheesy Christmas carols, the presents; everybody always seemed happier, especially if we were lucky enough to get snow.

In Fuerteventura there was no sense of any Christmas atmosphere at all. Rather than being wrapped up against the cold everybody was walking around in shorts and tee shirts and the island was still achieving temperatures of at least twenty eight degrees Celsius every other day.

Most of the shops, bars and restaurants were cashing in on the influx of tourists here for their Christmas break and we were just as guilty in the estate agents, attempting to sell half built homes off plan to maximise our own cash flow. I felt like a sleazy time share salesperson rather than a legitimate house seller but I shouldn't really complain, we were selling houses faster than they could be built and as a result it wasn't unheard of for sales reps like me to be taking home over ten grand a month. Still a bit of Christmas cheer would have been nice and, now that my loneliness had well and truly kicked in, I surprisingly found myself looking forward to Angie's imminent arrival at the start of next year.

In all of my thirty eight years I hadn't spent a Christmas alone and although I had received offers from people at work, and from Susan up in Corralejo, to spend Christmas with them I declined their invitations not wishing to intrude on their personal family time. I made a promise to myself that the same thing wouldn't happen to me again next year.

Next year I would aim to have the best Christmas of my life to make up for the miserable one that I knew was in store for me.

Just two weeks before Christmas I found out that the estate agency that I was working for was running a scam, they were taking thirty percent down-payments on houses that would never see the light of day as the builder had done a runner to Thailand. I immediately resigned not willing to associate myself with such underhanded schemes. I wasn't concerned about getting a new job as I'd already earned large sums of money in a short space of time so for the first time in a while I found myself unemployed.

CHAPTER TWENTY TWO

Christmas went by in a flash of insignificance. As far as I can remember it was the first time I missed the Queen's speech. I tried to Skype a few of my friends in the UK but the connection was too slow and wouldn't work. In the end I shut down the computer, made myself a couple of sandwiches and drove over to an isolated beach where I spent the day just watching the surf until it began to get dark. I returned home, showered and was in bed by nine o'clock that evening. New Year didn't fare much better either. Antonio and Simone were over in Italy for the holidays and it seemed as through almost everyone else on the estate was on holiday too. I watched the fireworks erupt at the stroke of midnight on the beachfront from the loneliness of my roof terrace, and vowed that this year I was going to find myself a man.

I barely recognised Angie as she stepped through arrivals that Wednesday night. Unlike most kids of her generation Angie didn't even have a Facebook page and I hadn't seen a recent picture of her for nearly twelve months. She'd gained weight but it suited her well, the last time I'd seen her she was all stretched out and angular, uncomfortable in her own skin. Now she looked relaxed and self assured, more feminine than I'd expected and the other obvious change was the lack of facial piercings. As she stepped through the barrier I held out my arms and drew her in close, her unique smell so achingly familiar it brought tears to my eyes.

"Angie, it's so good to see you," I whispered in her ear, still clinging tightly to her. "God I've missed you so much."

"Hi mum," greeted Angie pulling herself out of my embrace. "Can we get out of here, I'm desperate for a fag?"

I'd known that Angie had smoked for years but neither of us had ever allowed her to smoke in front of us, and it felt unreal as I took her wheelie suitcase from her and led her outside, while she casually lit up as if it was the most natural thing in the world.

"Is it always this hot?" she asked between drags as we made my way over to the parking pay station.

"No love, it gets far hotter than this, don't forget it's our winter now," I answered sneaking a quick glance at the digital thermometer mounted just above the pedestrian crossing behind us. It was only twenty five degrees, hardly what I would call hot.

After depositing the coins into the machine we headed over to my car.

"Is this piece of shit yours?" asked Angie.

I bit my tongue and agreed that it was.

Angie stubbed out her cigarette underneath her pink Converse trainer and climbed into the car.

"Jesus, it's even worse inside than it is on the outside," she said pulling at the foam stuffing inside my cracked, sun faded dashboard and sinking into the torn passenger seat ungratefully.

The urge to kick her out and make her catch the bus was almost overwhelming but I knew she was just testing the boundaries.

"So how are you? How's your dad and Marta? How are things back in England?" I asked.

"The answer to all three of your questions is shit. England's shit, dad and his fat girlfriend are shit and I'm pretty shit."

I waited for her to elaborate, but when she didn't, I attempted to bring the conversation back round.

"This here is El Matorral," I told her as we drove past the small village next to the airport. She looked disinterested out of the window. "If you look on the top of the hill over there," I said pointing to the hill on the right hand side, "You can see where my...where our house is."

"God this place looks awful, there's nothing here except dirt and rocks. I don't know why anybody would want to live here."

I'd forgotten how annoying Angie could be but I was getting a quick lesson. I knew I had a hard year ahead of me trying to ensure that mother and daughter would get along.

I showed Angie her room and surprisingly she seemed quite pleased with it.

"What do people do around here for fun?" she asked.

It was a question I hadn't anticipated.

"Go to the beach, swim, suntan, you know, stuff like that."

"Right, so there's nothing to do here except go to the beach."

"Well what is it that you want to do exactly?"

"Anything besides going to the beach."

"Right then, tomorrow we'll go hiking."

"You'll be hiking by yourself, why would you want to walk anywhere when you have a perfectly good car?"

"Oh, so now it's a perfectly good car, half an hour ago it was a piece of shit."

Angie shook her head and stomped upstairs to her bedroom, the door rattling in its frame as she slammed it behind her.

Strike one to Vanessa!

CHAPTER TWENTY THREE

For all Angie complained about living here I could tell that she enjoyed the freedom that she could experience away from the continuous pressure of her peers. Just as I had hoped to re-invent myself by moving here, Angie began to do that right before my eyes. I knew that one of these days she would have to get herself a job but in the meantime I was happy to let her take some time out to find her feet and as long as my finances remained stable then we should be okay for at least a year or so.

My book was sitting in the publishers awaiting its final edit with a tentative release date sometime towards the end of the year. Being a realist I knew I wasn't going to make a fortune out of it but if it could earn me enough money to continue writing then I would be happy with that.

Life was good but I still felt I was missing something. I wondered where all the good men were hiding. I worried about becoming one of those lonely spinsters with several cats that everybody crossed the road to avoid. I was still working out and swimming everyday and I knew I was looking good but time was catching up to me and the dreaded forty was just around the corner. I would have to attempt to find myself a man soon.

When Antonio arrived back from Italy without Simone at the end of January I consoled him as much as I could about the split.

"Maybe it's me, maybe there is something wrong with me that makes women finish with me," he surmised, tears pricking in the corner of his eyes.

"Well it didn't sound like there was anything wrong in the bedroom department," I said laughing.

"You hear us before?" he asked, his face creased into a frown.

"All the time...OH, OH, OH, SI, SI, SI, SIIIIII, AAARGH..." I giggled as I performed my best Simone impression. "She sounded like a porn star."

Antonio smiled ruefully.

"Why not us, why didn't we work out?" he asked suddenly serious, his eyes boring into mine with that hungry pleading look he knew I was always unable to resist.

I leaned closer towards him, our lips only millimetres apart when suddenly Angie rattled through the front door, her trainers squeaking down the stairs as she made her way towards the lounge where we sat guiltily shifting away from each other as that oh so close moment passed us by.

CHAPTER TWENTY FOUR

It's funny how things turn out but Antonio and I remained friendly but distant, the fleeting moment forgotten in the midst of time and I accepted that perhaps we were never meant to be.

Living right on the top of the hill left me isolated for long periods of time, especially since Angie had found a few friends with whom she would spend several days without returning home. I wasn't concerned about her being away, her friends came from decent families and Angie would always phone and let me know what she was up to but, until she started staying away, I hadn't realised how much I had depended on her for company.

I was dismayed when Susan from Corralejo had phoned me to tell me that she was returning to the UK with Hannah. Although we didn't see a lot of each other we spoke frequently on the phone and it was nice to know that I had a friendly shoulder to cry on if I really needed it. Mark and

Christine the piss head had moved in together and were at present growing twin goatees and bathing in vodka together according to Susan. Mark had somehow removed all of the funds from their UK account and Susan was returning home to her parents penniless after the bank had informed her that there was nothing they could do to return any of her money to her.

The week just gone had been particularly bad for me as Angie had been away almost all week, Susan was gone and Antonio had just started dating an Irish girl who'd just moved over to the island. I decided it was time for me to look for a job again, something to keep me occupied, somewhere where I could perhaps meet the elusive man of my dreams. With this in mind I drove into the capital and treated myself to some new clothes and two pairs of new shoes, stopping in at the salon for a trim and a new hair colouring. Well they say blondes have more fun. It was time for me to find out once again.

CHAPTER TWENTY FIVE

As far as job interviews go, this one rated as one of the most unpleasant I'd ever had to endure. The owner of the company spent the entire interview ogling my tits, now I know I have great tits but really, it was ridiculous. The owner's wife sat demurely alongside him while he spouted off the biggest pile of nonsense. The arrogance of the man was astonishing and he even had the cheek to exclaim that perhaps the job would be a little difficult for me, what with me being blonde. Every so often his mute wife would nod her head in agreement with him and smile at me nervously, her teeth a mouldy shade of yellow.

Although they both came across as unpleasant characters I really wanted the job. The work was easy, the pay was good, the office was air conditioned and just behind the desk was a huge one way glass window overlooking the hotel swimming pool. The lifeguard looked delicious.

The owner would be out most of the day which was a blessing and his computer illiterate wife would only come in once a day to collect the takings.

"That's all she's good for," he'd told me.

I would have plenty of time to start on my next novel and I would also finally get to meet people. The hardest thing I would have to endure was the boss undressing me with his eyes whenever he saw me.

When they phoned me that evening I immediately accepted the job. Lisa, the boss's wife, would spend the morning with me showing me the ropes and from then on I would be on my own.

I dressed carefully the next day, making sure that I wasn't wearing anything too revealing. I pulled a bulky sweatshirt over the top of my blouse even if it was a little hot to be wearing it. I looked in the mirror, pleased at how flat my chest looked in the unflattering top.

When I arrived at nine o'clock that morning the customers were already waiting. Jim and Lisa ran Si-Sidecars, a motorcycle and sidecar excursion company which was largely successful due to the novelty of the machines rather than the pretty basic excursions themselves. A loophole in the European licensing law meant that you were allowed to ride the motorcycles with just a car license and because each of the Russian manufactured motorcycle and sidecar combinations had been painted with a multitude of either football club colours, cartoon characters and international flags the bikes not only appealed to the kids but to the adults as well. I skirted my way past Jim with him barely noticing me and sat myself behind one of the two desks that furnished the office.

Lisa was busy checking licences and collecting cash but acknowledged me with a yellowy smile. I waited for Jim to finish his preliminary safety speech and for the bikes to leave.

"Hi Vanessa," greeted Lisa. "It's always such a mad rush in the morning but you'll get used to it." She pushed back her chair and made her way over to the coffee machine in the corner of the room.

"Coffee?" she asked.

"Sure, black, no sugar; thanks."

I took the thick black gloop from Lisa and she settled back into the chair next to me.

"Jim said that you're apparently quite good on the computer."

I nodded my head in agreement.

"Well he's asked me to ask you if you can set up a few fake profiles every morning that we can use for our Trip Advisor reviews. At the moment we're number one in the ratings of things to do in Caleta and we aim to keep it that way. What we do is send in at least two or three fake five star reviews per day. That way we can stay on top and get our annual certificates of excellence," she said pointing to the numerous framed certificates lining the wall.

"I can do that," I said, *but it's not right.*

"Once you've done that all we ask is that you answer the phone, take any bookings from the agents or people walking in and just log them into the diary. You'll also need to check our e-mails for reservations. You really have to be careful not to double book. This is a list of tours that we offer and the price list is here. Each driver has to have a full car license and on Sundays we only offer half day tours.

When Jim comes back he usually has about half an hour in the office to eat his sandwiches so if you have any major questions then ask him. If it's urgent then give me a ring, my number's here," she said pointing to a board with a list of mobile numbers, "otherwise all we ask is that you're nice to any potential customers, you don't use the phone unnecessarily and that you keep us at number one on Trip Advisor. Any questions?"

I shook my head.

"Right then, I'm off. See you at five, have a good day and sell lots of tours."

I couldn't believe how naive I'd been about Trip Advisor. I'd used it several times for holiday reviews blissfully unaware that it could be scammed so easily. I set up ten fake profiles that they could use for the next few days to spread their deceitful lies on the web and settled in, watching the lifeguard as he sat above the pool, unaware of the animal magnetism he was radiating through the one way glass.

Talk about a stress free job; only two customers entered the office before Jim returned with his entourage at around one o'clock.

"Hi Vanessa. How's your first day been so far?" asked Jim addressing my tits.

I guess it was my own fault; I'd forgotten to put my sweatshirt back on before he arrived.

"It's been quiet, I think. Only two lots of customers have been in but I managed to sell trips to both of them. I've also set up some fake profiles that you can use; they're on the desktop."

"Okay, thanks for that. We've got to do what we've got to do," he said shrugging his shoulders in a gesture that indicated that he was doing the whole world a favour.

"Technology is a great way to stay ahead of the game. When I ran my businesses in the UK we were always in the forefront of everything that we did and as long as you stayed that way then it was a license to print money," he said unwrapping his sandwich from its tin foil covering and taking a huge bite.

"Lisa can't see it," he said spraying crumbs over his protruding belly. "She never sees the big picture but I didn't marry her for her brains as anyone who knows her can tell you. She was blonde as well and she certainly lived up to her stereotype. If I left her in charge God knows what would happen to this business. Lisa doesn't care about this stuff, all she wants is her garden and, even though we live in a house worth over half a million, she's still never satisfied."

I listened to him waffle on, zoning in and out of the conversation, nodding or shaking my head like one of those nodding dogs you used to see in the back of cars back when I was a child.

After about ten minutes the new customers began drifting in for the afternoon tour. I was grateful for their intrusion if only because it got him to turn his attention to someone else and I was left to check their licenses and collect any outstanding monies.

That afternoon I started my new novel. I'd left my last book open ended so that I could utilise some of the characters from it in the new one. I realised that it was a lazy form of writing but my agent had suggested that I wrote it that way and she'd never been statistically wrong before, and when you looked at some of the authors that she had on her books, who was I to argue?

Before I knew it Lisa was back to collect the takings, check the diary and to make sure that I hadn't reduced their business to rubble in but a single day. I couldn't tell if she approved of me or not but the truth was, I didn't care. I certainly didn't take the job to become friends with either of them, in fact I couldn't even go as far as imagining anyone actually wanting to even be their friends, they were such an unlikable couple.

I returned that evening to my empty house and gave my Rabbit a quick buzz; the lifeguard in his tight red shorts the object of my masturbatory fantasy.

CHAPTER TWENTY SIX

On my third day at work I plucked up the courage to introduce myself to the lifeguard. His name was Juan and he was from mainland Spain. He seemed very distant and reluctant to talk to me but I persevered in the hope that it was just shyness and lack of confidence in his ability to speak English that made him that way. My perseverance paid off and before long he opened up to me and explained why he was being cautious talking to me.

It turned out that he'd had a major fall out with my boss Jim, something to do with one of the motorcycles, and Jim had threatened to sue him for misrepresentation of his company or something like that. Apparently one of Jim's favourite pastimes was threatening to sue people. He even did it with Trip Advisor. Whenever he would get a bad review, which was far more frequently than he would have you believe, he would immediately contact them threatening legal action if they did not remove it. He must have been the only person on the whole of Trip Advisor to have over five hundred five star reviews without a single bad one.

"Nobody in the hotel likes him," said Juan. "He is not, how you say?...He is a bad man." He tapped the side of his head in the universal symbol of madness. I guess I had him pegged from the moment I met him.

I arranged to meet up with Juan after gym, he went to the other gym at the top end of town, a basement dive frequented by ex convicts and steroid freaks. The sophisticated one I attended, a complete contrast with its full air conditioning, modern electronic machines and sea views.

We met at the local tapas bar around the corner from Juan's gym and spent a pleasant evening drinking cheap but delicious Spanish wine and sampling several strange dishes that Juan recommended and whose names I would never remember. We got along fine despite the language barrier and, although Juan possessed that certain *joie de vivre* that I looked for in a man, there was a lack of spark that was noticeable, despite the mild alcoholic haze that was beginning to blunt my senses and I knew beyond reasonable doubt that our relationship would go no further than mere friendship. When I returned home alone and stretched out on my double bed I worried that this was the way the rest of my life would pan out.

Angie was up and about when I got up the next morning, having returned home the night before.

"Where were you last night?" she asked handing me a fresh mug of black coffee.

"I was out on a date if you must know."

"Good, hopefully you'll finally get laid and I won't be kept awake by the buzzing of that vibrator of yours."

"Angie!" I felt myself flush a deep crimson "You can't talk to your mother like that."

"I'm just saying mum, there's no need to get upset about it. How's your new job anyway?"

"The job's okay but the boss is a bit of a dickhead."

"Yeah, I know your boss, I've met him a couple of times at Rachael's, her folks are friends of theirs. He's a right old perv, he was hanging out at the edge of the pool the whole time that we were swimming. I refused to get out until he went inside and I swear he only went inside to go and have a wank in the toilet. Listen mum, Rachael's mum's friend Jill has asked if Rachael and I would like to do some child-minding for this other couple that they know, they'll pay us and everything, it's just that they run a bar and they're hardly ever home and the kids are too young to go to school right now."

"But you don't know a thing about child-minding Angie, I mean do you even know how to change a nappy?"

"I know, but come on mum how hard can it be? Anyway Rachael knows how to change nappies because of her little brother and she can always show me."

"Well I suppose you having a job can only be a good thing and you can learn on the job." *It'll also be the perfect way to put you off having kids of your own too,* I though slyly.

"Oh and one more thing mum; we'll be living in their house."

"What? No Angie, there's no way you're staying at some strangers' house, you've only just turned sixteen."

"What's that got to do with anything? Rachael's mum doesn't mind her staying at their house and she's only fifteen." She pouted her lips angrily, the holes from her piercings clearly visible.

"Rachael's mum can do whatever she wants with Rachael but I'm not having you living away from home." I tried to stay strong and determined but I could feel my tears start to flow and I knew that once I'd started they would only get worse. "Shit Angie, you've made me cry," I started sobbing loudly.

Normally I would expect Angie to storm off in a huff, satisfied that she'd caused me to break down but she surprised me by taking me in her arms and hugging me tightly.

"It's okay mum," she murmured. "It's not like I'm leaving you alone. I'll come back home on weekends," she added, rubbing my back reassuringly.

I knew that there was something wrong with this picture and that it should have been me doing the mothering but I suddenly felt so vulnerable, so useless and unloved. Angie hugging me close brought all these feelings to a head and as I cried out my frustration I could feel what felt like a weight being lifted off of my chest. Everything was going to be alright. The chorus to Bob Marley's No Woman No Cry rocketed through my head in a reassuring mantra.

Everything will be alright.

CHAPTER TWENTY SEVEN

"Lisa tells me that you're a writer," said Jim.

I wished that someone would walk in and book a tour just to get him out of the office.

"Yeah I write a little. Girl's books really, you wouldn't be interested."

"Oh, but I would. I happen to like girls."

But girls don't like you, what was it Angie called him? An old perv!

"I was wondering if it would be okay for you to write up some of the reviews on our Trip Advisor page instead of just setting up the profiles. I'm sure with your writing skills we could create a whole new level of interest," he said trying to butter me up.

God, if he was any more transparent he would be invisible.

"I'll give it a go," I answered, "but I must warn you, I'm not that type of writer."

"It's alright, I trust you'll do a good job, I mean, what are we paying you for really? You get to sit around and do whatever you want to do on the internet all day so it's not like I'm asking too much of you."

Inside I was seething but I ignored his attempt to justify asking me to do his dirty work as I'd just had a great idea. He was so going to regret asking me to write his reviews.

As soon as he left the office I began my first review.

We took our trip with Si-Sidecars on the 4th of July, Independence Day in the good old US of A and I chose the bike with the stars and stripes in honour of the day. My wife kept referring to my son Jaden and I as bad boys because of our black leather jackets and jeans but Jaden made it clear that we weren't bad boys we were the coolest ever men in black. Whenever I'm on holiday I'm always in the pursuit of happyness and I knew as soon as I saw the sidecars parked up outside Si-Sidecars that they would be the type of vehicle in which I could quite happily hitch a ride. When we first set off on the motorcycle I was amazed by the terrain, it looked like something out of the wild, wild west and I kept expecting cowboys to come herding over the hills. All in all it was a great day and it was worth spending the extra seven pounds on the fantastic DVD of the ride. Thank you Jim.
Will & Jaden Smith
Bradford, West Yorkshire.

I laughed as I posted the review onto Trip Advisor knowing that Jim would just see it as another five star review and that he wouldn't even realise what I had done.

In the space of one review I'd managed to use the titles of seven Will Smith films. *Independence Day, Bad Boys, Men*

In Black, The Pursuit of Happyness, Hitch, Wild Wild West and Seven Pounds, and to top it off I'd signed off the review as Will Smith and his son Jaden.

Boy was I going to have fun with these reviews!

I spent two more hours writing reviews from dead rock stars, writers and even an artist. It was fun really and I was dying to find out if anybody picked up on it on Trip Advisor. When Jim returned from the bike shop later that afternoon I showed him my work and he was pleased as punch.

What an idiot!

CHAPTER TWENTY EIGHT

At around eight thirty that night there was a knock on my door. Antonio and his new girlfriend Sinead were standing there hand in hand.

"Come in," I said stepping aside to allow them access.

They followed me down the stairs and into the lounge.

"You want anything to drink?"

"Just a glass of water," answered Sinead, in her soft Irish lilt.

"Nothing for me," Antonio said.

I didn't know Sinead really well but she seemed a nice enough girl and she wasn't a screamer, which I took as a huge bonus after putting up with Simone's nightly racket.

"So what brings you guys around?" I asked as I handed Sinead her water.

"Two things really," said Antonio. "First of all we're getting engaged," his eyes flashed in happiness.

I swallowed hard, my mouth felt dry and I thought that I

might throw up.

"Congratulations, I'm so happy for you guys," I lied. I got up from the couch and hugged them both.

"And we're leaving Fuerteventura; we're moving to Ireland next month."

I felt as though Antonio had just driven the final nail into my heart. I tried to force a smile but it felt wrong, all crooked, like my teeth had been glued to my lips.

"That's great," I croaked. "I'm going to miss you guys so much. What brought on the move?"

"Sinead likes it here don't you?"

Sinead nodded in agreement.

"But she feels as though she's just treading water. There's no jobs over here for skilled people and she's worried that if she stays here too long she'll lose her skills and her brain will turn to mush."

"I can understand that, but what about your business?"

"Well I've managed to find a buyer for it so Sinead leaves for Ireland in two days time and I'll be following her at the end of the month, once I've shown the new guy how everything works," he said. "We're going out for a meal with a few friends tomorrow night and we wanted to ask you if you would come along?"

"Of course I will," I said. "Wow, I can't believe so much is happening all at once."

As I saw them to the door later that evening I knew I only had two and a half weeks in which to get Antonio to change his mind.

I couldn't let him leave me here alone!

CHAPTER TWENTY NINE

I endured Antonio and Sinead's going away dinner by getting completely smashed. Only close friends were invited which meant that the most of the guests were Antonio's friends as Sinead hadn't really formed any major friendships on the island in the short time that she had been here. With nearly all the guests native Italians it left just Sinead and I as the English contingent. Everything was free and the red wine was irresistibly fruity and before I knew it I'd polished off nearly two bottles of the stuff. Sinead and I bonded that night and drunk as I was, I knew that I didn't have it in me to attempt to steal Antonio back from her. Besides, she was far closer to his age than I was.

On Monday morning, just after Jim had left on the sidecars and I was alone in the office, a man walked in asking for Jim.

"I've just finished doing some work on one of the bikes for him and I need to collect some cash."

The Russian bikes were always breaking down so I didn't see this as unusual, however I knew that this wasn't the regular mechanic that Jim usually used.

"I'm afraid he's just gone out on tour and won't be back until at least one o'clock," I answered.

"Do you mind if I wait?" he asked settling into the couch opposite the desks.

I didn't really know what to say. It would be a good three hours before Jim returned and I didn't want to phone him unnecessarily whilst he was leading a tour, but I couldn't understand why someone would wish to wait that length of time in the office. I glanced over at him sitting forward on the couch waiting for my answer. He had this air of desperation about him yet he seemed relaxed enough and by no means creepy enough for me to contemplate phoning the police just yet.

"Sure, if you're prepared to sit and wait. Do you fancy a coffee?" I asked moving from behind the desk to the coffee machine.

"If you're having one then I will," he answered. "I'm Rick by the way."

"Vanessa," I said shaking his hand.

He was quite good looking in a non convention way. When he smiled I noticed that one of his front teeth was pushed back slightly from the other giving him an almost childlike cheeky grin and that his eyes were a sparkling emerald green contrasting sharply with his dark hair. He looked better when he smiled, although it looked as though he wasn't really used to smiling that much.

I handed him his coffee.

Nice 'n Sleazy

"Milk and sugar are over there," I said, pointing to the Tupperware containers next to the machine.

He stood up to get some sugar and I was surprised that I hadn't noticed how tall he was earlier. I felt slightly uncomfortable when I returned to my desk, I was hoping that perhaps he would at least start some sort of conversation to cut the atmosphere but he didn't seem forthcoming and, in the end, I felt obliged to at least engage him in conversation, if only to acknowledge that he was there.

"So Rick, I haven't seen you around Caleta. Have you been here long?"

"Not really," he answered. "I moved over here to start a business a couple of weeks back, just after me and the missus split up. I'm in limbo at the moment, waiting for the courts to decide how much I'm supposed to pay her and until they decide that then all my accounts are frozen and I'm stuck without any cash, hence me doing odd jobs to keep myself going."

He had a strange accent, part West Country, part Northern, like someone who moved around a lot until all the regional accents blended into one.

"Surely the courts will allow you a bit of cash to keep you going until they reach a result," I said.

"You'd think so yeah, but my ex missus, she's such a bitch and because I have a multi million pound company in England she's trying to take me for everything, the houses, the cars, the boat; everything."

"She sounds like a nice lady," I said sympathetically.

We spoke while we waited for Jim to return.

Rick had done a lot in his life. He'd been an airline pilot, a nightclub owner, a mechanic, a motorcycle racer and now he was in the scrap metal trade. He owned three houses, one in London, one in Devon and one in Leeds. The two houses in the south had indoor swimming pools and the London one was valued at over five million pounds. I loved that although he claimed to be a rich man he was still very down to earth. There was nothing designer about him and even his unshaven look didn't seem pretentious. He seemed nice but somehow damaged, like the divorce was really hurting him badly. I wondered if I could find a place in my heart for this sad man.

That night I knocked on Antonio's door and invited him over for something to eat. I knew he would be missing Sinead and I wanted to tell him about Rick.

"I don't like the sound of this man," said Antonio spooning the last of his pasta into his mouth.

"You're just jealous," I said laughing.

"No, seriously Vanessa. If you're a multi millionaire you aren't going to be rolling around on the floor fixing those crappy bikes of Jim's and come on, a pilot, a racer, I don't believe him. I think he's full of shit."

I felt stung by Antonio's words. I'd wanted him to be happy that I might have actually found a man worth falling in love with and here he was questioning someone he'd never even met.

"One thing you have to remember Vanessa is that this island often attracts bullshit people. If this man has three houses and a yacht then why isn't he living in one of those until the courts decide how much he has to pay? I'm telling you chica be careful, I think this guy's come over here to try and scam people, and he's hoping his bullshit story about being a millionaire is going to make people fall all over him."

"He doesn't seem like that at all and if he's scamming people then why is he doing work for them?"

"He does it to gain their trust. If you meet someone who's prepared to work hard for a few euros you can easily be fooled into thinking that he's an honest hard-working man. Once you believe that then he's more or less halfway there; before you know it he'll be borrowing money, your car, even moving in with you all on a false promise that one day he'll pay you back, with interest, for the kindness you've showed him. Watch him carefully if you meet him again and you'll see what I'm talking about chica, I don't even know the guy but I'm telling you, he's just a con man."

I was disappointed in Antonio's lack of faith in humanity and was grateful when he bid me goodnight and returned next door. Not five minutes after Antonio left I heard the keys rattling in the door as Angie returned home for a rare visit. She looked exhausted and seemed to be losing weight.

"Are you okay love, you look knackered?"

"I tell you mum, I didn't realise how much hard work children could be. I'm never having any of my own if I can help it."

I made her a mug of hot chocolate and, before she'd even managed to finish it, she was fast asleep on the couch. Rather than wake her I fetched a blanket from upstairs and covering my baby up gently, I left her sleeping.

CHAPTER THIRTY

I met Rick five days later once again in the Si-Sidecars office. He stuck around long enough to invite me out for a drink that evening, explaining that he had work to do and that he was already running late. I readily accepted and was looking forward to it. I promised myself that I would take into consideration Antonio's warnings but I still felt that he was wrong and perhaps he was, like I was with Sinead, a little jealous.

We met at one of the dimly lit Irish bars located upstairs, away from the hustle and bustle of the high street. Inside it was quiet and our table next to one of the windows afforded us a splendid view of the tourists rambling below.

Rick looked good in his buttoned down white shirt and faded blue Levi's and as he pulled back the chair for me to sit, I was both surprised and impressed by his old fashioned display of manners.

"I've never been in here before," I said as Rick took his

place on the opposite side of the table.

"It's like my local," said Rick offering one of his rare smiles. "Pat, the guy who owns it, lets me keep a tab here until some of my funds are released."

Straight away warning bells began to ring and I thought back to what Antonio had said to me a few nights back. I tried to push their persistent ringing out of my mind, as I didn't want to spend the whole evening evaluating everything that Rick said, but it was obvious that Antonio had tainted any time Rick and I spent together.

I asked for a vodka and lime rather than red wine. The problem I was finding with the wine just lately was as soon as I started on it I tended to go overboard and I wanted to ensure that I kept a clear head throughout the date. I didn't want to end up doing something that I would immediately regret in the morning.

Although I enjoyed the date, I found that Rick wasn't much of a conversationist and try as I might to banish Antonio's warnings from my mind I couldn't help feeling that perhaps Rick was hiding something.

When Rick asked me back to his apartment for the inevitable clichéd coffee I accepted not for any other reason than to see where it was that he lived.

"It's not a bad place," he said as he busied himself making coffee. "And it's only temporary, hopefully the funds will be ready for my golf course villa soon."

I smiled to myself thinking how much of a full circle life sometimes takes you. Here I was drinking coffee in the apartment next door to the first apartment that I'd ever lived in here on the island. After coffee I made my excuses and called a cab to take me home. I was pleased, yet disappointed, that Rick hadn't hit on me on the first date.

Did he think I was not good enough for him?

CHAPTER THIRTY ONE

I woke up on Saturday morning with the inexplicable urge to dance. Once I got to the office I phoned Rick and asked him if he wanted to head up to Corralejo to go clubbing. He disappointed me by refusing claiming he never danced unless it was deemed absolutely necessary so I quickly dropped Antonio a text asking him if he was up for it. He sent me a text back almost straight away saying he would be happy to go out with me. Surfing the net, I found us a cheap hotel room with twin beds and made the necessary arrangements.

It had been ages since I'd been to The Reflex and I was looking forward to not only dancing, but to getting out of Caleta for a while. When I got home I packed my pyjamas and picked out my dress for the night, the same little black number as the one in the poster. This time I would at least be wearing stockings and suspenders. At five o'clock that evening Antonio and I set off in my little car to Corralejo.

"Have you seen that guy, what was his name Roy, no Rick, have you seen him lately?" asked Antonio.

"Yeah we went out on a date the other night. He seems quite nice."

"And what did you think about what I said to you? Do you think maybe he's a con man?"

I'd thought about it a lot and the truth was, I did harbour a slight suspicion that something wasn't quite right but I couldn't bring myself to commit to accepting that Rick was over here on false pretences and, until something was proved beyond reasonable doubt, then I refused to be the one to judge him.

"I don't know Antonio, you can interpret everything that people say however you want and twist it to sound like something else. Look at all the variations of ideas that claim to be inspired by The Bible, look at the way lawyers can twist things to suit their own gains. I don't know, I think he's just an unhappy man trying to get away from his wife who just wants to get along without people judging him all the time. Anyway forget about Rick, tonight we're going to party like it's nineteen ninety nine!"

Antonio flashed his wicked grin. "You never know chica, perhaps you'll even get me dancing tonight."

As we passed the red mountain and headed into the dunes I felt a pang of nostalgia for the time I'd spent in Corralejo. The turquoise sea and white sand was awe inspiring when you hadn't seen it for a while and it was a great reminder as to why we chose to live on the island. I wondered how Antonio was feeling knowing that he only had a week left here.

"I'm going to miss this," he murmured, gazing out of the window dreamily.

"You'll come back for your holidays won't you?"

"I'm not sure if I will. I've enjoyed my time here, but there's so much more of the world to see and it seems a waste coming back to the same place time after time. Sinead wants to go to India and I wouldn't mind going to China after I've seen Mexico and also I have to go back to Italy to see my family every so often so if I come, I come. If I don't you can bet I'm having a good holiday somewhere else. Maybe one day we'll come back to live, who knows?"

I liked his attitude. So many people lived their entire lives so cautiously and before they knew it they were suddenly old and full of regrets for the things that they hadn't done. Although a lot of people I'd met here were not the type of people I'd choose to hang out with, at least they were equipped with a sense of adventure and when their time came they could at least say that they did it, even if they happened to do it gracelessly and with little sense of style.

CHAPTER THIRTY TWO

The Reflex was jam packed to the rafters. I noticed someone handing out flyers for the club near to where we parked the car and was surprised that they were still using the image of me to promote the club. Antonio pocketed one and promised me that he would treasure it forever. Although I still looked similar to the girl in the photo, my new hair style hair ensured that you would be hard pushed to recognise me. The truth was I didn't care if I was recognised or not, the inhibitions that I secretly carried around with me like unwanted baggage were cast aside the moment we left Caleta. I'd come here to party and to say goodbye to my former lover and one of my best friends, and that was exactly what I was going to do.

I felt liberated and exhilarated to be here and I wondered if perhaps I should return to Corralejo on a permanent basis once again if only to regain this unexpected feeling of euphoria. Entering the ladies toilets immediately caused me to change my mind as I watched three young girls, barely eighteen, taking turns at snorting lines of coke in one of the open stalls. It would seem that, after the relative calmness of Caleta De Fuste, Corralejo wasn't quite the type of place to bring Angie to.

Rather than letting the blatant drug use spoil my evening, I ignored the goings on that surrounded me and just let the music bring me back to the time in my life when living was simpler, yet more confused. I danced until even my legs ached and by some sort of miracle I also managed to get Antonio to bust a few moves.

By the time we returned to the hotel I was exhausted and I collapsed into bed fully clothed allowing Antonio to remove the shoes from my feet.

I was asleep the moment my head touched the pillow.

CHAPTER THIRTY THREE

I hadn't spoken to or seen Rick since our date and I felt I needed to see him more than ever. Antonio was leaving in a few days and I knew that when he left I would need a shoulder to cry on once he was gone.

When Jim arrived back from his tour I casually asked him if he knew where Rick would be.

"He'll be up in that Irish bar that he drinks in, what's it called, The Harp or something like that? What do you want him for?"

"No nothing really, I know this guy that might have some work for him," I told him, not willing to divulge my personal life to Jim of all people.

After work I tried the bar but he wasn't there so I made my way over to his apartment and knocked lightly on his door.

What if he was with another woman?

He opened the door in just a pair of shorts, a distracted

look on his face. He offered a fleeting smile, his green eyes questioning.

"Hi Vanessa, what can I do for you?" he asked, his half naked body blocking the doorway.

"Aren't you going to invite me in?" I enquired boldly.

"I would do but the place is such a mess I'd prefer not to. Give me two minutes and I'll pull on a shirt and some jeans and we can go over to the pub," he said closing the door on me gently.

I waited in the corridor for about thirty seconds before I decided to leave. As I turned towards the staircase Rick came bounding out of his door, catching up with me.

"Where were you going?" he asked me, a hurt look on his face.

"I don't know, anywhere, I've never had someone slam a door in my face before," I replied angrily.

"Vanessa, I didn't slam the door in your face, I just didn't want you to come inside that's all. It's not like I invited you over and believe me when I tell you the place is in a mess, then it really is in a mess. I've got lots of personal documents spread out all over the floor, bank account statements, business accounts and God knows what else. Surely I'm entitled to some sort of private life!"

I couldn't believe that Rick had twisted it so that it was me that felt like the guilty one. I walked alongside him my heels clicking angrily on the concrete paving slabs.

"I got some good news today," he said forcing a smile. "The lawyer is supposedly releasing some of my funds in the first week of next month so I'm going to buy myself a car to run around; I've been thinking about getting one of those new Porsche 911 convertibles. I've got one of the older models in the UK and it's such a nice car but I know she'll end up getting it off me as part of the divorce settlement. Do you think you could take me to the showroom in Puerto Del Rosario sometime next week after work to go and look at one?"

I felt a flush of excitement at the thought of going shopping for a brand new Porsche.

"Sure Rick, just let me know when you want to go."

"Perhaps we can see how the finances are and we can replace your car with something a little nicer like a Porsche Boxster."

Rick certainly knew the quickest way to a girl's heart!

I knew as soon as he mentioned buying me a Porsche Boxster that I was going to sleep with him. It's not like I hadn't intended to sleep with him but I had at least hoped to take it slowly, to get to know him first, but prostituting myself, *could I call it that?*, for a Porsche Boxster with a guy I found better looking with each passing moment seemed a small price to pay. And I was horny as hell.

After two hurried drinks at the bar I invited him back to my place for something to eat, whispering a silent prayer that Angie wouldn't be home.

As we ate I could feel the sexual tension in the air, in all our spoken words and all our unspoken gestures and I don't think I'd ever been as eager for sex before without any sort of foreplay. I shifted in my seat and I could feel the seam of my jeans rubbing against my damp swollenness like an expert lover. Standing up on wobbly legs I felt the beginnings of a squirming orgasm as I dragged an equally eager Rick into the darkened bedroom like a primitive cave girl.

The moment we entered my bedroom I was practically begging Rick to fuck me and I managed to achieve multiple orgasms for the first time in my life in the space of less than five minutes.

I'd like to report that Rick was a great lover but I don't think he really was. The build up had been so intense that it made it seem that way but when it came around to doing it again he seemed uncertain and lacking in confidence, even struggling to maintain an erection.

I worried that I'd frightened the life out of him with my first performance and that things would never be the same again between us and that Rick would be impotent around me from now on.

Fortunately this wasn't the case and when I woke the next morning with his stiffened cock digging into my side I knew that taking him gently into my mouth would be the best way to ascertain that everything was functioning correctly and I can happily report that it was.

I went to work with a smile on my face and was unusually nicer to the customers than normal. Jim noticed straight away.

"Why are you so happy this morning Vanessa?"

"Well it's nearly the end of the month and I'm getting paid soon."

And you're going out shortly and I'll have the office to myself.

Well at least I thought I would but Jim was back around half an hour after he'd set off.

"You tell that fucking Rick with a P if he ever steps foot in this office again I'll personally flatten him," he exclaimed.

"What's happened Jim?"

"We've just had a major accident because of that twat. He was supposed to have changed the brake pads on the Man United sidecar the day before yesterday. So the customer comes to a junction pulls the brake lever and nothing. He goes straight through the junction in front of a delivery van. He's broken his right leg and his right arm and his daughter has broken her wrist and cracked some ribs. His wife's a bit shook up but she's okay. They could have been killed. Anyway the police and ambulance and everything come over, the police close the road and the traffic department accident investigators turn up taking photos and everything and guess what? They discover that the brake pads are down to the metal, nothing left of them at all and that twat was supposed to have changed them. I mean I paid him to do the job and everything. Now we've got a bike written off, the possibility of a huge fine and two people in hospital because of him. Fuck, I really don't need this shit."

"Are you sure it was the same bike that Rick fixed?"

"Of course it was, do you think I'm fucking stupid?"

"Fair enough," I replied raising my hands in submission.

I knew that there would be no comeback on Rick because he wasn't legally working on the island and I was sure that there would be a reasonable explanation as to why he hadn't changed the brake pads, but I have to admit that once again those warning bells were ringing.

Maybe, just maybe, he wasn't everything that he

appeared to be.

Lisa came in and piled up a bunch of documents for Jim to take over to the police station. The insurance cover was only third party and as the accident was caused by one of the sidecars then Jim and Lisa were responsible for all of the damages.

As soon as they left I tried unsuccessfully to phone Rick but he wasn't answering his phone. I needed to at least let him know what had happened so that he could defend himself if the need arose.

I only saw him again on the night when Antonio left for Ireland when he turned up unannounced outside of my door, suitcase in hand and dripping blood from both his nose and from a number of nasty cuts beneath his beautiful green eyes.

It seemed Antonio might just have been right all along.

CHAPTER THIRTY FOUR

I led Rick into the bathroom and, wetting a clean towel, I set about cleaning up his battered face. Usually, when someone is bleeding quite badly, once they are cleaned up you discover that the wounds are superficial but this wasn't the case with Rick. Whoever had hit him had been wearing some sort of huge signet ring and each punch that had landed on his face had caused deep lacerations that refused to stop bleeding.

I suggested I took him over to the hospital but he refused to go and asked me instead to go and find a spider's web.

I thought he must be concussed or delirious or something but he told me that if I collect up some of the spider's thread it would stop the bleeding. Apparently it was something he'd learnt as a child from a gypsy woman. I headed outside to the numerous cactus plants I had growing in pots in search of a spider's web and managed to return to the bathroom with a handful of the sticky silvery thread.

Quickly Rick wiped at one of the bleeding wounds and scraping a blob of web from my hand onto the end of his finger he inserted the web into the wound. The bleeding stopped immediately. He repeated this procedure on all the other wounds until he was no longer bleeding at all. I was astounded that it actually worked and told him that he should bottle and patent it.

He grinned through split lips at my suggestion and began to explain what had happened to him.

"You know I'm supposed to be buying one of the villas on the golf course,"

I nodded my head.

"Well the estate agent that was selling the place, I don't know if you know him, John Creswell,"

"Everyone knows John Creswell; Tenerife Mafia," I interrupted.

"Yeah well, he told me I could live in the apartment I was in rent free until the cash came through for the villa. A couple of days back he started harassing me for the money and told me I had twenty four hours in which to get it or I would have to move out. I explained that it wasn't up to me, but it was up to the courts, but he wasn't having it and he warned me that if I didn't get the cash there would be serious consequences. I tried all yesterday to get the lawyer to release some funds, just enough at least for the deposit but the court wouldn't budge and I couldn't get the money together in time. Anyway the two Steves turned up and this is the result. Now I've got nowhere to stay and John

Creswell has told me I need to give him a thousand euros by tomorrow or else he will smash up both of my hands with a sledgehammer."

He began to cry, his bruised face streaked with blackened spider webs, dried blood and now fresh tears.

"We need to go to the police," I said to him.

"We can't go to the police. He owns the police. If he finds out I've gone to the police, which he will for sure, he'll kill me. I just need a thousand euros to get him off of my back until my money comes through next week."

"Wait here," I said exiting the bathroom and making my way downstairs to my safe.

I counted out a thousand euros and took the money upstairs to Rick. I had a strong sense that I was being played but I didn't know what else to do. John Creswell was not a man you crossed lightly and there were rumours of numerous bodies buried all over the island that had his name on them. I didn't want to be responsible for Rick's disappearance.

I watched those green eyes light up as I handed him the money.

"Now go and pay the man," I said. "You can leave your suitcase here."

"Thank you Vanessa. Thank you so much, you don't know how much this means to me; You're a life saver."

He pocketed the money, kissed me on the cheek and promised he'd be back as soon as he'd paid John Creswell.

I never saw Rick again.

CHAPTER THIRTY FIVE

The rumour mill that is Caleta De Fuste was in full swing the following week and Rick was the talk of the town. Apparently Rick had done over the owner of the Irish bar for eight hundred euros, John Creswell for a thousand euros, Jim, my boss for three hundred euros and God knows how many other people. Thankfully, nobody knew that I had given him a thousand euros and I wanted it to stay that way; I didn't want people thinking that I was a desperate and gullible fool. I didn't even tell Antonio when I spoke to him on Skype as I didn't want him saying I told you so. When he asked me about Rick I simply told him that he'd decided to go back to the UK.

Sinead and Antonio had got engaged in a little tavern in the local village where Sinead came from and it had taken Antonio two days to sober up afterwards. He'd now more or less given up drinking completely and was even talking about giving up the cigarettes mainly due to the price of them over there. He'd secured a job as a telesales person for a large machinery company where his three languages could be put to good use. He loved everything about Ireland besides the cold. I missed him terribly and his being away made me realise how few friends I actually had here on the island.

I decided it was time for me to make some new friends and when Jim and Lisa invited me over to their house for a barbecue on Friday night this time, instead of declining their invitation, I gladly accepted in the hope that I might meet some new people.

I returned home that night determined to change my life. I started with the last remainder of my past, Rick's battered suitcase was still sitting unopened in the corner of my bedroom.

Drawing it toward me I released the catches. I was surprised to find an airline pilot's uniform inside. I studied the insignia but the truth was I didn't know what I was looking for and it was only when I saw the sewn in label proclaiming "Made in China" that I realised that, unless he was a pilot for some Chinese airline, it was a fake. There were only three other items within the suitcase, an old plain white tee shirt, a pair of surf shorts and the most scary of all, a seven inch long dagger with a silver handle.

I snapped the suitcase shut and dragged it down to the rubbish bins, tossing the whole thing into the bin.

Rick was history.

CHAPTER THIRTY SIX

The Friday night of Jim's barbecue I decided to dress up a little for the occasion. I chose a pale blue strapless mini dress along with some killer heels I'd bought in the capital at a closing down sale. I suppose I was still looking good, but I'd been slacking a little in the gym and I needed to get back into a proper exercise routine, instead of trying to fool myself that the reduced amount of exercise that I was doing would really keep me in shape.

I found Jim's villa situated in a row of similar villas on one of the roads leading off the golf course. As I parked my car up I could hear the sound of voices raised over the music coming from behind the gate. I pushed the bell and the sound of a dog's barking interrupted the merriment.

"Shut it Pablo," called Jim opening the gate, his left hand clutched tightly around his large dog's collar. "Well look at you Vanessa, come on in. Don't worry about Pablo he's all bark and no bite. Be careful of the step there," he said pointing downwards. "Let me introduce you to everybody."

I met several nice people that night, but unfortunately the crowd was dominated by couples and the few men that were single were closer to Jim's age than mine. I did however meet Erika. I was drawn to her as soon as I laid eyes on her. She was the type of girl that the term Supermodel could have been coined on. Close to six foot in her heels, her blonde hair literally sparkled in the spotlights that Jim had installed around the entertainment area. You couldn't help but to be drawn by her beauty and I was surprised that she was standing to one side alone. I introduced myself to her, startled by the intense blue eyes that met my gaze. Erika was just a couple of years younger than me and hadn't been on the island for long. She didn't know Jim at all and had tagged along with a friend. We hit it off immediately, it was like we'd been friends for life and by the end of the evening I'd invited Erika to move in with me. At the moment she was renting a room from a friend of a friend and she didn't really get on with the other tenants. It was perfect for me as not only did it provide friendship and company for me but it also justified the extra rent that I was paying for a two bedroom house which was more or less surplus to requirements since Angie had moved out. Any stuff that Angie had left behind I could always move into my room.

Erika, like me, was also single but she wasn't on the lookout for a man, in fact she wasn't interested in men at all. Erika was a lesbian. I'd met a few lesbians over the years but the ones I met were usually the butch, dungaree wearing stereotypical lesbians. Erika didn't look anything like that at all and if she hadn't been straight up with me and told me before she moved in I would never have known. I quite liked the idea that my new flatmate was a lesbian; finally I was meeting some real-life interesting characters which I could perhaps utilise into my new book.

I hated to admit it, but the book had almost ground to a halt and I was really struggling to find the inspiration to keep the thing going. If my editor hadn't suggesting using characters from my old book I don't think it would have progressed anywhere near as far as it had done and the few new characters that I had introduced seemed shallow and superficial to me. I needed to invent someone big and bold, someone that my readers could relate to. Perhaps a lesbian protagonist would be the way to bring the book out of the quagmire of fluffy slushiness.

Although Erika wasn't working she had a business plan that she wished to utilise over here and whilst she was explaining the details to me she suddenly hit on an idea.

"Why don't we become business partners?" she asked. "It'll work much better if we run it together and you can still keep your job at Si-Sidecars."

"But I don't know anything about...about those things," I answered, pointing to the suitcase full of sex toys that Erika had brought down from the bedroom."

"What's there to know; some of them you stick in, some of them you strap on, some you just wear, it's all quite obvious really and think about it Vanessa, there's not one person on the island doing these parties and come on, everyone has sex don't they? Even if it's by themselves," she added with a laugh. "We'll make a small fortune."

I couldn't quite imagine myself as a purveyor of adult sex toys but I knew that there was a market for them out there; the mileage my own Rabbit had done over the last few months could vouch for that.

I told her I'd sleep on it and let her know the next day.

CHAPTER THIRTY SEVEN

I lay awake that night unable to sleep, Erika's business proposal running through my head. I'd always been quite inhibited with regards to my sexuality and it was only when I became separated from Jeff that I realised that I too could actually demand sex when I felt like it. Roger, the man down south, had taken me to new heights that I was willing to explore further with the right partner and even the boldness of buying my own sex toy online had been a brave move on my behalf. Now look at me, here I was sharing a house with an outgoing, hot looking lesbian, who planned to turn me into a sex toy salesgirl. I tried to imagine the scandal that it would have caused back in my village in the UK.

I awoke that morning excited by the decision I'd made. Erika and I were going to become business partners and I was going to become a party planner. Erika was already in the kitchen and handing me a cup of tea she looked at me expectedly.

"And?" she asked.

"Yes I'll do it. We're going to have to advertise it in all the local free papers and some of the bars, I know, perhaps we can have an open night at one of the bars and we can sell the stuff from there. There's plenty of bars that'll be happy to have our trade, especially a bunch of women playing with naughty underwear and vibrators. We could make it a weekly feature..." I rambled on excitably hardly giving Erika a chance to get a word in edgeways.

"Steady on girl, don't get your knickers in a twist, we can't do anything until we get some more stock," said Erika. "The stuff I have here right now are just samples and if we're going to sell to people you have to get them at the spur of the moment before they change their minds. I had thought about setting up an order list but the problem with that is the person makes the order and then the next day realises she can live her life without those Chinese balls or those anal beads so she cancels. You have to have the stock on hand if you're going to make a living out of this."

I sipped at my tea, ideas still flowing around in my head.

She continued, "We're also going to have to set up a website where the more shy ones can buy their stuff online..."

I flushed guiltily thinking about my own online purchase.

"...And we have to come up with a name that's slightly naughty but girly enough not to scare the punters away. Oh, and we're going to have to train you up as a party planner and host. You need to know how everything works and you'll have to be prepared to demonstrate for those women not quite bright enough to get it."

"What do you mean by demonstrate?" I asked. "I'm not getting my bits out in front of strangers."

Erika laughed loudly.

"I can tell you've never been to one of these parties before Vanessa. They can get slightly out of hand if you know what I mean"

I left for work wondering what the hell I'd let myself in for.

We chose the name Nice 'n Sleazy because it summed our business up perfectly. Erika loved the name as apparently it was the name of an old Stranglers song and back in the day Erika had been a bit of a punk.

The evening was spent pouring over the supplier's catalogues arguing over which items to order. I was quite happy with the usual stuff like furry handcuffs, vibrators, lube and sexy underwear but when it came to the more extreme stuff I felt quite uncomfortable - I mean skin-tight rubber masks, nipple clamps and butt plugs, just who was going to buy those things here in Fuerteventura? Erika agreed that the more usual stuff would sell better than those which I considered extreme, but she assured me that there was a market for the other stuff too and insisted that we had a healthy enough supply to cater for all tastes.

CHAPTER THIRTY EIGHT

Angie turned up at my workplace the next morning with a tall dark skinned boy and the two kids in tow. I was pleased to see her as it had been a while since her last visit. She seemed to be growing up more day by day and I was constantly amazed at how her temperament had done an almost u-turn from the way she was when she first arrived.

"This is Aziz," she said.

Aziz smiled nervously.

"Pleased to meet you Mrs. Wilson."

"Please, just call me Vanessa; Mrs. Wilson sounds like an old lady."

Actually I am an old lady compared to him.

Angie and I spoke about general things whilst Aziz kept the kids entertained outside. I told her about my business plan with Erika and Angie seemed decidedly shocked which both surprised and pleased me no end.

"So is Aziz your boyfriend?" I asked.

"Mum," chastised Angie squirming in her seat and turning a deep shade of red.

"What? I'm only asking. He seems a nice enough boy," I said. "You are on the pill aren't you?"

"Mum, God you're so embarrassing, of course I'm on the pill."

I changed the subject and when they said their goodbyes I realised that I'd never sat down with Angie and had the mother – daughter birds and bees conversation. I knew that it was too late in the game to do it now but I still felt guilty that I had ended up doing the exact same thing as my own parents had done, simply ignoring the subject of sex and I vowed to make it up to her sometime soon. I wasn't naive enough to think that there was much I could teach her, in fact I wouldn't have been surprised if there were things that she could have taught me, but I was sure that if we could sit down mother and daughter and discuss any concerns that she may have, it would bring us even closer than we had become.

I pondered on how all of a sudden sex had become almost a domineering feature in my life.

Hah, if only I was getting some!

CHAPTER THIRTY NINE

I returned from the printers with a huge box full of flyers, posters, gilded invitation cards and order forms. I could hardly contain my excitement, Nice 'n Sleazy was becoming a reality! All we had left to do was to contact the free papers and magazines to book a place for the advertisement we'd designed. All of the new gear was sitting at customs waiting for us to pay the import duties and taxes, which I planned to do later in the evening and then we would almost be ready.

Our grand opening night was to take place in a fortnights time at one of the pool bars that a friend of mine Jackie owned. We'd set up a Facebook page and, in the space of three weeks, we already had close to five hundred members. We'd sent out electronic invitations for the opening night and over a hundred and fifty women had confirmed via the RSVP button that they would be in attendance. I'd even invited Jim's wife, Lisa. It had all the makings of a great and hopefully lucrative evening, not only for Erika and me, but for Jackie as well.

A hundred and fifty drunken women let loose with a multitude of sex toys. We were going to need shares in Duracell.

When I went to collect the boxes from customs I could tell that everybody in the office was aware of the contents of the supposedly discreet boxes. It seemed like every man and his dog had crowded into the open plan office for a glimpse of the girl with a thousand sex toys and my face felt like it was permanently blushing.

I handed two of the Spanish flyers out to the only women in the office and they smiled at me knowingly. I'd explained to Erika that we needed to break into the Spanish market and she thought that she might have somebody interested in the job so she planned to train both me and the new girl at the same time.

Once I'd paid everything, two strapping young lads helped load the boxes into my car. I swear they must have drawn straws to undertake this menial task and I wondered if I simply snapped my fingers and pointed to one of the guys that weren't helping me, if he would come bounding from behind his desk like a puppy dog, eager to please.

How naive of me not to realise how much power sex had over men.

When I got home Erika helped me unload the boxes and we placed them in the middle of the lounge floor, opening each individual box and crossing the products off of our comprehensive list.

"My God, what is this?" I asked Erika, holding up

something torpedo shaped but wider than both my hands put together.

"That my dear is the mother of all butt plugs."

I felt myself pale.

"No way! There's no one alive that could get that up their butt and, if they managed somehow, they wouldn't be alive afterwards. I don't think either of my kids were that big when they were born."

It took us three hours to itemise everything we'd bought and to put it into some semblance of order and my insides ached with the laughter we'd shared. Some of the stuff was just so ridiculous it brought tears of laughter to both our eyes. I couldn't believe I'd allowed Erika to buy a complete skin-tight rubber suit complete with a gas mask.

"Just who in hell's going to buy that?" I asked almost choking with laughter.

"Oh no that's not for sale, that's for me," she answered with an evil grin.

Okay... Now I was very worried about my training this weekend.

CHAPTER FORTY

Bianca, the Spanish girl that Erika had found for the job turned up at the house at around seven thirty that Saturday night. She looked very young and innocent and I was surprised when I found out later that she was already thirty two and had been married twice.

"Right girls, first things first; uniforms."

Erika handed the two of us plastic bags with our uniforms inside. I started heading towards the stairs but Erika yelled at me to come back.

"We're all friends here, we get changed here in the lounge."

"That's not fair, what about a uniform for you?" I asked sulkily.

"Don't worry, I'm going to be wearing one too."

Bianca twisted her denim mini around and began unfastening the buttons as if this was something that she did daily. Taking her cue I began removing my clothes and before long both of us were stood nervously in our underwear.

"It's all got to come off ladies," ordered Erika who quickly stripped out of her clothes, standing naked before us.

I dutifully stripped off and we removed our uniforms from their respective packages. The underwear was absolutely beautiful, some sort of fine silky lace so soft to the touch it felt as if it wasn't really there at all, and the almost translucent knickers with each of our names embossed in a red velvet heart across the front were simply fantastic. The uniforms too were exquisitely put together French maid outfits that clung to our bodies as we moved like a second skin; the soon to become legendary Nice 'n Sleazy emblazoned in a fine metallic chrome scroll over each of our left breasts.

"Erika these are outstanding. Where did you get them from?"

"I know a girl who studied clothing design at college and she sourced the material from all over the place, the silk used on the bras and knickers is from hand reared silk worms in China, the lace is made locally by a half blind old lady and the material for the uniforms is sourced from France and from Italy. These things were specially made just for us and cost a fortune so look after them. Oh and watch this."

Erika reached down to the velvet heart on the front of her knickers and peeled it back leaving her most private parts exposed.

"I'm thinking of adding something like this to our

catalogue but I know you wouldn't believe me if I told you that these things cost over eighty euros a pair. I'm not sure how many people would be willing to part with that sort of cash for a pair of knickers," she said pushing the heart back in place.

"I like this," said Bianca in her slight Spanish accent, placing two of her fingers over the ANCA of her name leaving just the word BI.

Ah, so that's how Erika found Bianca!

Six bottles of wine and two packs of wet wipes later all three of us were physically worn out. I'd done things that I wouldn't have thought of doing to myself in private, let alone in front of these two girls and any shyness I'd previously had with regards to sex and to my body had dissipated with each sex toy we tested. We'd began by testing the different vibrators firstly on our tongues, moving on to our nipples and then on top of our underwear and as the wine continued to flow the more daring we became.

Erika and Bianca had the unfair advantage of knowing each other intimately previously but it didn't take long for me to loosen up, our sex toys had a way of doing that to you, and before long I found myself with an eight inch long vibrator with a rotating rippled end buried deep within me, right in front of my business partner/ best friend and a girl I'd only met that evening. It hadn't felt sexual as such, just us girls having a laugh and it wasn't as though I'd suddenly decided to go batting for the other side over some tipsy mutual masturbation and I can truly say, hand on heart (my real heart not the one sewn on my knickers), that we had some mighty fine adult toys available from Nice 'n Sleazy. I also knew that without a shadow of a doubt our opening night was going to be a night I'd never forget.

When I woke up on Sunday morning I didn't know if I'd even be able to look Erika in the eye but when she joined me in the kitchen I surprisingly felt relaxed and not in the least embarrassed.

"That was a right laugh last night wasn't it?" asked Erika, pushing her tussled bed hair back from off of her face.

"It certainly was. God, can you imagine what next Saturday's going to be like?"

"All three of us are going to have to work it, oh yes please," she said as I pointed to my tea cup. "It'll probably be easier to split everyone up into groups of three and that way we won't be shouting at everybody."

"Are we going to let everybody test drive the stuff like we did last night?" I asked thinking mainly of the hygiene issues involved.

"Yeah we have to really, that's what these parties are really about, letting these sexually stifled housewives discover a whole new side to them that they didn't even know existed before they came to our party. We're going to need a shit load of batteries, some of the more complicated vibrators use quite a lot of juice, no pun intended," she said grinning. "And wet wipes; we're going to need boxes of those. I'm not sure how Saturday will go, to be honest with you; the biggest party I ever went to was only thirty people and they were all friends, I couldn't even begin to imagine what's going to happen when over a hundred and fifty sexually charged strangers get together."

"We'll just have to take it as it comes," I said. "Most of

the women over here won't have ever been to one of these parties so they won't really have any great expectations. Do you think we'll have enough samples to go around?" I handed Erika a slice of toast, the butter melting rapidly into the toast the way she liked it.

Erika took a large bite of the toast and followed it up with a gulp of tea before answering.

"Maybe, maybe not; as long as we don't have any cat-fights over whose turn it is next to use the Big Boy dildo or something like that I don't care. At the end of the day we've got at least a hundred different samples and some of them are never going to get used at all, I mean take that huge butt plug you showed me the other night, not unless this party gets well out of hand will that get anywhere near to being used and if it did, man I would love to see that. You might find hardly anyone tries anything out at all, that's where we step in and show them how it's done. It only takes one person to set the ball rolling and before you know it you've smashed through those barriers, and any inhibitions those women were once burdened with will be gone if not forever then at least for that evening. It's all about timing, you've got to get them at just the right moment. If you get that right we'll walk away needing to order a hell of a lot of new stock, and that's what we have to aim for. You have to remember that we're not doing this for love or to improve Mrs. Brown's sex life; we're doing this for money. This is a business, a fun one perhaps but it's still a business. We've spent over ten thousand Euros on stock and the most important thing is for us to see a return on our investment."

And there was me criticising Antonio when he told me that the island was a great place to make money yet here I am, a corporate whore; literally! Don't you just love irony?

CHAPTER FORTY ONE

Natalie phoned me on the Sunday night and asked if she could come over to Fuerteventura on Wednesday, just for a week's holiday as she needed some time apart from her current boyfriend. She'd found several cheap flights available on the net for that particular day. I explained to her that, because I had someone living with me now, I would have to make sure that she was okay with it first and that I would ring her back as soon as I'd discussed it with her.

Erika was easy going as a rule so I was sure that she wouldn't have a problem with it but I still had to make sure that she was happy having Natalie sleeping on our shared sofa.

Natalie always seemed to be having problems with her boyfriends and often, when she was going through one of her numerous rough patches, I would feel guilty that I'd left her behind to deal with things herself. I knew that her father wasn't much use at all and, as for his fat Polish bitch of a girlfriend, what did she know about relationships anyway?

Erika was more than happy for Natalie to come over and was looking forward to meeting her

"If she's coming on the Wednesday night that means that she can come to the opening party," Erika said.

"Ha, not likely, I'm not having any daughter of mine coming to one of our parties,"

"Why not, it'll be fun and she'll be so proud of you," Erika reasoned.

"You mean she'll be so embarrassed that she'll want to die. Could you imagine watching your mum demonstrating sex toys whilst dressed in a French maids outfit and semi-crotch less knickers? It would scar her for life; I know it would have me. Angie would just shake her head laughing at me and let me get on with it but Natalie, Natalie will freak out. I haven't even told her about Nice 'n Sleazy and I'll try and keep it that way."

"Surely Angie will tell her won't she?"

"Natalie and Angie don't really get on, at least they never used to, and to be honest, I think even Angle's a little embarrassed by the whole Nice 'n Sleazy thing so I don't think she'll be telling Natalie what we're doing. In fact I get the impression that Angie thinks that you and I have got something going on. She hasn't exactly come out and said so but I can tell the way that she looks at me. I don't know; call it mother's instinct, but she's definitely suspicious."

"Does it bother you that your daughter thinks you're gay?"

"I'm not saying that she thinks I'm gay. I think she thinks I'm going through an experimental phase and that I'll get over it eventually. She's been through so many experimental phases in her life that I suppose she expects everybody else to do so themselves."

"Really; has Angie ever gone through a gay phase then?"

"Angie, ha, no chance of that, I'm surprised she's even got a boyfriend."

I explained to Erika how Jeff and I used reverse psychology to try and keep Angie away from boys, and how Angie hadn't even had a boyfriend until she moved out of home.

"My mum figured out really early that I had a thing for girls," said Erika. "It didn't concern her too much because as far as she was concerned at least girls couldn't get you pregnant. It was only as I got older and she figured out that because I was a lesbian I wouldn't be giving her any grandkids that she started becoming involved in my sex life. She'd try and set me up on dates with men which I attempted to go on just to get her off of my back. They were some of the most horrendous things I've ever had to endure."

She laughed at the memory.

"I'd never had sex with a man and there was this one guy, God I can't even remember his name, Andy or Alan, I don't know, I think it started with an A. Anyway he seemed kind of nice, you know me, I'm not a man hater but there are a lot of dickheads out there," she paused and you could see her face soften as she was transported back to that time.

"We'd gone to this vegetarian restaurant. I was going through one of those hippy phases at the time; hey I guess Angie and I are alike in some ways, going through our phases. Anyway this Andy or Alan or whatever his name was, he was quite switched on. We liked the same music, the same films, we'd read the same books; we even shared the same political outlook. Basically he was a male version of me. What I liked about him was that he wasn't too manly, you know like those grizzly, hairy men you used to see in those old cigarette and shaving ads. His skin was clear and looked quite soft, I wouldn't call him feminine, but if he turned out gay later in life I guess I wouldn't have been too surprised. Anyway I'd had quite a lot of sex with other girls, you'd be shocked by how many straight girls have had girl/girl sex before, so I thought okay, this guy seems kind of cool maybe I should have sex with him just to be able to say that I'd at least given it a fair chance," she paused for breath and I could tell that this was something that Erika hadn't told that many people before.

Erika's revelation about straight girls and gay sex suddenly brought on a flashback that I'd sort of repressed; taking me back to when I was fourteen and we were round at my parent's friend's house in Devon. It was summer time and it was a warm evening, I remember that I was surprised that it was still as bright as daylight at around nine thirty at night.

Debbie, my parent's friend's daughter had set up a tent down the bottom of her garden and we were sitting inside it discussing boys. She was a year younger than me and fancied one of the boys in her class but didn't know how to approach him as she'd never had a boyfriend before. I'd had a boyfriend or two but nothing serious, all we'd ever done together was hold hands and share a few fumbling kisses but with me being a year older than her she expected me to be much more worldly wise than she was with regards to the opposite sex.

Debbie's biggest fear was kissing a boy. She'd seen French kissing in films and had practised using her tongue on her hand but she couldn't tell if she was doing it right using her just her hand. I told her not to worry, it would come naturally but I could tell that unless she knew for sure that she could do it properly then she would never build up the courage to even tell the poor guy how she felt. I knew that we were leaving Devon the next day and heading back to Wales and I liked Debbie and felt kind of sorry for her so I suggested she tried practising kissing me.

I taught her to let her lips just touch his gently then to slowly open her mouth whilst their lips were still touching.

"Don't go sticking your tongue down his throat straight away, let him make the first move but if he doesn't just push your tongue gently into his mouth and lick at his tongue, just a few gentle flicks, I guarantee you he'll respond to that," I'd told her as if I was some sort of expert.

She'd leaned towards me and did what I told her to do. She was a quick learner and before long our tongues were twisting together like it was the most natural thing in the world. It was Debbie who pulled us apart after a particularly intense three minute kiss and I could see the confused look of longing in her face. I knew how she felt because I felt the same way too. Remembering this I realised that had Debbie taken our kissing to the next level back then I would have most certainly have let her; in fact I remember masturbating quietly in my hotel room that night after we'd left their house, wishing it was Debbie's fingers instead of my own pushing and probing deep inside me.

Erika interrupted my reminiscing.

"So we finish our meal, which was awful by the way, I'm never going vegetarian again, and I suggest to him that he comes back to my place so we can listen to a few records, maybe share a joint or two and I can tell he's nervous as hell but up for it."

I sat listening to her tale, spellbound by her storytelling and all the glorious details. Erika, unlike many other lesbians I'd met, didn't really dwell on her sexuality hugely and I took it as a privilege that she had chosen to open up to me. Even though Erika's story seemed to be all over the place, you could tell it was coming up to a great climax and as a writer I knew I was getting some fantastic material here.

"I'm sure I'd put The Buzzcocks record on because it was probably the most romantic music I had back then. Isn't it funny that I remember The Buzzcocks but I can't remember the guy's name? I suppose back in those days I was still into setting the mood. God no wonder the guy was so nervous, he probably thought I wanted to marry him or something."

I laughed along with Erika, trying to picture a younger, less confident version of her alone with a boy for the first time.

"I rolled us a joint, it was probably about ninety percent tobacco but I was hoping it would take my nerves away, but more so that it would relax him a little; the poor guy looked as though he was going to suffer a stroke or at the least throw up the vegetarian slop we'd eaten earlier. Anyway I didn't really know where to start so I just leaned over and began to kiss him. I remember we were kissing and he had his arms straight down his sides not knowing what to do with them. I thought to myself this isn't really working so while I was still kissing him I grabbed hold of his hand and pushed it inside of my bra,"

Erika began laughing so hard tears were flowing down her face. I laughed along too simply laughing at her infectious laughter.

"You won't believe it..." she began laughing again unable to continue.

"He came in his pants."

We both shrieked with laughter.

"He came in his pants from touching my tit."

My first time was equally funny but not funny in the sense that Erika's was amusingly funny; mine was just funny how things had worked out. I was kind of naive about sex but I was friends with a bunch of bikers who lived next door to us. I was like their little sister and they would do small but useful things for me, like fix a puncture on my bicycle and just generally make sure that I was alright when my folks were out drinking or were fighting. I remember them affectionately as a bunch of long haired dirty guys, they were always covered in oil and even today the smell of oil brings me back to Hilltop Road and the time I spent there.

I was fifteen years old so I wasn't exactly a child but I think in this day and age they would have all been arrested and put on the sex offender's list just for allowing me to hang around with them. Danny, the main guy was heavily into pornography. The house was littered with tatty porn magazines and the only time I ever saw the old black and white television set switched on was when Danny and his friends were watching a porn film, so I was naive about sex, having never had sex, but I knew how it was all supposed to work.

Davey had just left school at sixteen to become an apprentice bike mechanic. I'd known him from school so when I'd seen him in his overalls downtown one day we got chatting and I told him that I lived next door to one of the chapters of a notorious motorcycle club. He was really impressed that I knew Danny and the boys and he invited me out to the cinema that weekend. I can't remember the film at all as we spent the whole time snogging in the back row. I knew that my folks would be over at the club when I got home so I invited him back to my house on the condition that he would have sex with me. I'd been wanting to lose my virginity for so long, it seemed like I was the only virgin left in the school, but the only guys that I knew well were the bike gang next door and they were way too old for me to even consider letting them near me.

We went up to my room, I can still see it now, my pink eiderdown and white pillows with pink sunflowers on them; a little girl's room, and I asked him to undress first. He tore of his tee shirt and began unbuttoning his jeans before I'd even had a chance to remove my shoes.

His erection was pointing towards his white belly and I couldn't resist the urge to touch it. I took his firmness in my hand and it pulsed and jerked like it had a life of its own before it erupted like a fountain, his thick white cum running down the back of my hand and my arm. Following the example of one of the porn films I'd seen at Danny's I'd licked it all off of my skin, catching the remaining drops with the ends of my fingers of my other hand, all the while watching his reaction. I then popped my fingers into my mouth one by one and licked them clean.

I thought he was going to faint.

Worried that if we did it while his cock still had cum on the end of it I would fall pregnant, I took his still erect cock into my mouth and sucked as hard as I could, hoping to get rid of all the spunk inside. Once I'd done this I let him put it inside me and all I remember was that it hurt like hell and was thankfully over very quickly.

Nine months later Natalie was born.

The only people who knew about Davey were my parents and Danny the main man from the biker gang who I'd confided in. Davey never worked again, Danny saw to that, and the last I heard of Davey he was a burnt out junkie living in a squat in Cardiff. I don't even know if Davey knew that he had a child.

As for Jeff, I'd met him whilst I was pregnant with Natalie and he took on the role of father to her when she was born. Even Natalie doesn't know that Jeff wasn't her real father and neither of us, even now we're apart, has any intention of ever telling her otherwise.

CHAPTER FORTY TWO

Natalie looked tired but still fabulous when I picked her up on the Wednesday night. She hugged me tightly for ages without saying a word. When we drew apart I could see that she'd been crying.

"I've missed you so much mum, God you look great, I would hardly have recognised you." She reached in her pocket for a tissue and dabbed gently at her eyes.

"You look great too love. Your hair's grown so long since you were last here. Here, let me take your suitcase."

I extended the handle out and pulled Natalie's suitcase behind me like a subservient dog as we exited the arrivals lounge into the dusky half light.

"You've still got your old car I see," said Natalie as she climbed into the sagging passenger seat."

"Yeah I don't need much more than this. I mean I know someone here who bought a brand new car about four months ago and it already has about four or five dents on it where people have just crashed into it and driven off. It happens all the time here so, at the end of the day, you're better off having something like this because then you don't spend your whole life worrying about your car every time you park it up."

"So mum, tell me about this woman you have living with you."

"I think you'll like her, she's really pretty, quite stunning actually and she's really easy going. She's not far off my age but looks way younger,"

Natalie interrupted me.

"Don't put yourself down mum; you look young enough to be my sister."

"Why thanks darling, *I am young enough to be your sister!* Anyway she's got long blonde hair a lot like yours and she's, well...She's a lesbian."

I watched Natalie pale.

"Are you, you know are you and her...?"

"No, no, nothing like that love, we're just great friends. She's a really cool person and I know you'll get on well with her, she's dying to meet you," I said hurriedly.

"Phew, that's a relief, I couldn't imagine having to tell people I had a lesbian for a mum."

How was I going to explain Nice 'n Sleazy to Natalie? She was so conservative!

As we turned to go up the hill it began to rain, just a light drizzle, but it was the first time I'd seen it rain since I'd lived here. It had rained but only at night whilst I was sleeping and I always woke up feeling disappointed that I hadn't seen it coming down. I marvelled at the smell of the damp earth permeating through the car. Switching on my windscreen wipers, they squealed out in protest at being woken from their semi-permanent hibernation. My dusty windscreen soon turned into a blur of mud and the wipers seemed to be successfully making it even more difficult to see.

"Lucky we're nearly home," I said to Natalie as we turned into the communal driveway.

As we approached our house I caught a glimpse of Erika in the headlights dancing on the pavement in the rain dressed only in a bikini.

"Who's that nutter?" asked Natalie pointing at Erika.

"That my dear, is the woman I live with. That's Erika"

CHAPTER FORTY THREE

Although I may have had slight apprehensions as to how Natalie and Erika would get on I shouldn't really have been concerned about it at all. They got on so well that I was left feeling like a third wheel whenever we did anything together as a threesome. It was only on Saturday morning that Natalie opened up to me and told me what had been troubling her.

Natalie was pregnant.

She was only eight weeks on and unless she'd have told me I would never have noticed. She'd only found out three days before she'd phoned and asked if she could come over. When she'd told her on/off boyfriend Carl he'd slapped her across the face and told her to get rid of it because it probably wasn't his. She'd gone home to her father in tears and he'd told her that there wasn't room in their lives for a baby.

"If you're thinking of keeping it then you've got two

choices," he'd said her in no uncertain terms, "you'll have to go live with your mother or you'll have to move out."

"I can't believe you'd kick your own daughter out of home," she'd screamed at him.

"What makes you think you're my daughter anyway?" he'd bellowed back at her.

"What's that supposed to mean?" Natalie had asked.

"Ask your fucking mother," he'd replied.

I felt physically sick. How could Jeff do this to Natalie? She was as close to his flesh and blood as you could get without planting the seed. He'd been present at her birth, her first tooth, her first steps, her first words, her first day of school, her broken arm when she'd fallen from the climbing frame in the local park; he was as much a part of her life as I was, if not more since I'd left for Fuerteventura.

We'd made a vow on the day that she was born that Natalie would always be his daughter, regardless of anything that may happen to us. I couldn't believe he could be so heartless. I hated him more than I ever had for what he had done to Natalie and now I hated myself for what I was going to have to tell her.

Coming clean to Natalie was destroying everything that she'd ever believed in and I knew how difficult it all was for her to take in. There were tears and anger and even shock when she realised that Angie wasn't her real sister but, considering how long we'd hidden the truth from her, she handled it far better than I would have expected. It was a lot to take in.

"I was only sixteen when you were born, I was just a child myself and I'd only done what I thought was the best for you". This was the best that I could offer and I knew that under the circumstances I probably sounded weak and pathetic but it was the truth; nothing more, nothing less.

"I understand how traumatic this must be for you mum, me telling you that I'm pregnant and you having to tell me something that you would never have expected to ever have to do. I know why you did it though and although I'm still a little confused about everything right now, I just want you to know that I still love you."

We hugged and cried and hugged again and when she asked about her real father I told her all that I knew.

The weird thing was, I didn't even know what Natalie's father Davey's surname was. I offered to hire a private investigator to find him if she wanted but she wasn't really that interested.

"As far as I'm concerned," she said pausing to blow her nose. "Dad is still my dad even if he isn't my dad if you know what I mean. I mean I'm twenty two now, and I don't need to make friends with some junkie waster just because he happened to take advantage of my mum when she was just an innocent teenager. He would have been locked up nowadays. I think we should tell Angie the truth though."

"Well love I'm sure you've earned the right to choose how you want to handle this situation and if you want us to tell your sister together then we will but can we please do it tomorrow? I don't want to sound selfish or anything but tonight is a big night for Erika and I and we've got a lot of organising to do."

"I know mum, Erika told me all about it..."

"She did," I said surprised.

"Yeah, she said that you'd be far too scared to tell me. I don't know why, but she's showed me quite a lot of the stuff that you're selling and I think it's great mum; your own little enterprise, I'm proud of you mum and I'll be cheering you on tonight."

My first born daughter is going to a sex toy party hosted by her mum! Shit!

If you'd have told me that Natalie was going to be present at the Nice 'n Sleazy opening night just a few hours ago I would have refused to do it, but now that I was unburdened by the huge secret I'd been carrying around for what felt like most of my life I suddenly felt closer than ever to Natalie and I would have been disappointed if she wasn't there; I needed her support as much as she needed mine.

CHAPTER FORTY FOUR

Erika dressed in her French maid outfit came out onto the makeshift stage and up to the microphone to cheers and screams like a rock star. We followed close behind, Bianca standing to her left as I positioned myself on the right,

Nice 'n sleazy, nice and sleazy, does it, does it, does it every time, blared The Stranglers from the speakers positioned on both ends of the stage. I was so nervous that I could feel my legs shaking. I grinned as I spotted Natalie near the front of the stage, cheering along with the rest of the women. One hundred and seventy one women were crammed into every available space, and you could feel the heat and smell the concoction of intermingling perfumes radiating from the crowd below.

"Good evening ladies," announced Erika.

"Good evening," chorused the audience.

"Tonight is about us women. For too long have we been

suppressed by traditions and so called moralistic values. For too long have we been told how to behave both in and out of the bedroom. For too long have we been giving and not receiving what is rightfully ours."

Wolf whistles and cheers rippled through the crowd. Erika worked the crowd like a natural.

"Orgasms ladies, that's what tonight is all about; good old healthy, earth-shattering orgasms."

Erika paused and turned to look at me as everyone cheered. I smiled encouragingly.

"Well tonight ladies we're going to claim what is rightfully ours, we're going to embrace our inner selves and treat ourselves to something we've been denying ourselves for far too long. We are going to show you how the earth can move for you and you alone. How often have we, regardless of our sexual orientation, given our partners orgasms beyond belief only to be denied one in return? No longer ladies, no longer are we going to accept mediocre, from now on we want, NO, let me rephrase that, we demand our fair share of pleasure..."

I wondered if Erika should perhaps be in politics rather than wasting her time as a sex toy salesperson.

"And if, like me, you are single, or if your partners' aren't up to the job we are going to show you one or two things that certainly are. Tonight ladies we're going to introduce you to your new best friend, a friend that doesn't talk back or turn over on its side and fall asleep, a friend that is always there for you whenever you're up for it and a friend that is indeed always up for it. Ladies my name is Erika," she said pointing to her name tag on her crotch, "and this is Bianca and Vanessa and together we are Nice 'n Sleazy."

We bowed together as one on the stage before I switched places with Erika at the mike.

"Ladies we're going to split you up into three groups if that's okay. I'd like you to draw an imaginary line from this table here," I said pointing to the left hand side of the crowd, "And from that table over there," I continued, pointing to the right hand side of the crowd. "Behind me I have a range of samples of all sorts of pleasure giving sex toys from simple thimble clit massager's to butt plugs of extraordinary proportions. Now ladies I hate to bring this up but hygiene is of utmost importance here. At the end of the stage and on every table you will see packages of wet wipes. Please we implore you to use them regardless of what you are doing with some of the toys. I suggest trying the vibrators on the end of your tongue rather than using them the way that they are intended to be used but if you do get the urge to try them out properly who are we to stop you, after all you came here for fun didn't you?"

Everybody cheered and I relaxed a little.

"Bianca, Erika and myself will be circulating and answering any of your questions and if any of you wish to place an order, don't be shy, we're here to help. Oh and I almost forgot," I said distracted by Bianca handing me a fifteen inch long clear dildo. "Before we start proceedings we still have the Deep Throat Competition to judge, so if I can have those of you who put their names down for it up on stage now please."

Nine women of differentiating ages and sizes made

their way to the front of the stage, once again to huge cheers from the crowd.

"What we have here ladies is one of our Big Boy clear latex dildos, a bargain at a one off special price of thirty euros for tonight only. The ladies here at the front of the stage have entered our Deep Throat Competition to win a Nice 'n Sleazy gift hamper to the value of one hundred and twenty euros. The gift hamper consists of everything a girl needs for a good night in and they make a great gift for that special friend or if you just want to pamper yourself and can be bought from any of the three of us here tonight. The rules of the competition are simple. The lady that swallows the most wins the hamper. Please remember to give each of our contestants a big hand as they come on stage, and without further ado, can we please have our first contestant up on stage, contestant number one is, let's see, Emma from right here in Caleta De Fuste."

Emma stepped up on the stage and taking the dildo in her hand she sank to her knees to rapturous applause as she tilted her head back and pushed the dildo straight down her throat. Erika knelt alongside her, marker pen at the ready, as more and more of the dildo rapidly disappeared down the petite girl's throat. Just watching her brought tears to my eyes but the crowd loved it and that was the most important thing. By contestant number six, Emma's eleven and a half inches opening shot was the one to beat and it wasn't looking likely that anyone would top that until contestant number seven climbed upon the stage. The first thing she did was pull out her false teeth placing them next to her onto the stage. The crowd erupted with laughter and everyone began cheering her on, standing on the tables and chairs to get a look at her as she swallowed the dildo inch by inch until there was just enough room for her fingers. Contestants number eight and nine conceded defeat without even attempting to beat Carmel from Northern Ireland's incredible feat. Luckily there were no men here because believe me; some of these ladies here certainly knew how to make a man feel inadequate.

The evening was a resounding success and, by the time the three of us got home at just after two in the morning, Natalie was exhausted and headed straight to sleep on the couch, but Erika and I were still too pumped full of adrenaline to even think about sleeping. We sipped at mugs of steaming hot chocolate whilst we counted the money we'd made, stacking it in neat piles on my bed.

"Four thousand seven hundred and sixty euros in one night," said Erika in amazement.

"Minus the product cost plus Bianca's pay of a hundred euros, that equates to a profit of three thousand one hundred and seventeen euros but that doesn't include the fifty six euros we've spent on wet wipes and batteries, oh and the hamper, we need to minus off another forty five for that," I said, switching off the calculator.

"There's no need to get technical really," said Erika, "just call it three grand profit; that works out that on average each woman spent twenty eight euros. I wonder how much Jackie made at the bar."

"Probably as much as we did in profit I reckon. Perhaps we should charge bar owners to host our parties to make a bit more cash."

"Ha, look at you Vanessa, a proper little corporate whore. I don't think it's a good idea, you want to stay friendly with the bar owners and charging them to host your parties will just piss them off. I think we need to promote Nice 'n Sleazy in Corralejo and set our sights on getting a party going up there. There's even more people up there so we should do even better than we did here. The thing is I don't really know Corralejo at all and I know Bianca doesn't because she's from the south."

"Leave it to me," I said, "I know just the place!"

CHAPTER FORTY FIVE

I slept 'til midday on Sunday, then after a quick shower I rang Angie and arranged for her to meet us at the beach café where we could grab a spot of brunch. I was nervous about having to tell Angie the truth about Natalie's father but nowhere near as nervous as I had been when I'd had to tell Natalie. Besides, Natalie would be offering me support and as she had taken it so well I couldn't really expect Angie to be as upset as Natalie was, after all at least Angie knew who both her parents were.

Angie was late for our meeting and we were halfway through our food before she eventually turned up looking the worse for wear, a huge bruise on her cheek and a swollen black eye.

"My God Angie, what happened to your face?" I asked in horror.

"It's not as bad as it looks," she said. "One of the kids pushed a swing into my face when we were in the park yesterday," she answered taking turns at hugging the two of us.

"We were starving and couldn't wait any longer so we started without you. Do you want something to eat?" I asked.

"No thanks I had breakfast earlier, the kids always have us up at the crack of dawn, I'll just have a Coke."

I studied my youngest daughter in the bright sunlight flooding through the café's windows and realised that she had lost even more weight than she had the last time I'd seen her. The truth was, she actually looked quite ill.

"Are you sure you don't want just a sandwich or something, you're looking far too skinny nowadays?"

"Look, just leave me alone okay, I'm not hungry."

"Okay love, whatever you say."

It was Natalie who told Angie about her getting kicked out of home for being pregnant and how she'd discovered that Jeff wasn't her real dad. I just nodded my head in agreement where necessary as the two of them spoke. I was worried about Angie, she just didn't seem herself and her obvious disinterest in the whole Natalie affair didn't help alleviate my concern about her well being at all.

I started to worry about what a bad mother I'd turned out to be, my youngest daughter, only sixteen, living in a house more or less on her own and me, totally unaware of any of the goings on there, I mean I'd only been around there once since she'd moved in. It was time I paid more attention to the well being of my daughter.

Suddenly I had a terrible thought. What if it was that boyfriend of hers, Aziz that inflicted the damage to her face? I longed to ask her but was afraid of the rift that it would cause between us. I would have to think of a way around finding out more about the boy. I mean he seemed nice enough but no one really knows what goes on behind closed doors and I wouldn't want my baby girl caught up in an abusive relationship.

Even though Angie knew about my party the night before she didn't ask about it and when Natalie told her about some of the goings on she just offered a strained smile, downed her Coke then told us that she had to go.

I was very worried indeed.

I expressed my concerns to Natalie when Angie left but she told me not to worry, that Angie was just being Angie and that the next time we saw her she would be totally different. It made me feel a little better but it wouldn't stop me from attempting to find out more about Aziz, I was sure that one of the two Steves would be able to help me, they knew everything there was to know about absolutely everybody in Caleta and what they didn't know they could usually beat out of them.

Before I knew it, it was Monday and I was back at work. It was Jim's birthday and I'd bought him a huge tin of Quality Street that he could really have done without. He seemed to be getting lazier and fatter month on month. He'd employed a new driver called Martin who, although young and enthusiastic, wasn't really gifted in the brains department. Jim would spend more and more time in the office on his computer or else popping around the corner to the bar, where he would sink at least three or four pints before returning annoyingly drunk. Once he was in this state he would either spend the whole time taking the piss out of Martin, if he happened to be in the office and, if he wasn't, he spent the rest of his time studying my tits and slagging off his dim witted wife.

He retired to the pub earlier than usual using his birthday as an excuse and when he arrived back even more inebriated than normal he started directing his abuse at me.

"Word in Caleta is you like a bit of this," he said holding his fingers in a V shape and flicking his tongue between them. He stood up swaying and begun unbuttoning his shorts.

"I bet it's been a while since you've seen one of these," he said exposing his short stubby cock.

"One of what," I asked innocently.

"One of these," he said tugging at his cock in a feeble attempt to try and make it appear bigger.

"I'm sorry Jim, I can't see anything. I don't know what you're talking about."

"One of....Ah, I get it, ha ha" he slurred, his semi-erect sad and emaciated cock hanging pathetically out of his trousers like a naughty schoolboy.

No wonder Jim's wife Lisa had been one of the first of our customers to buy the Big Boy dildo. I'm sure Jim's limited appendage would have struggled to touch sides.

"Listen Jim, you're drunk and I'm going home now, I'll be in tomorrow to collect my outstanding pay and my holiday entitlement and I'd just like to tell you that you can stick your job up your fat hairy arse."

I made a few keystrokes on the computer and snatching up my bag I left him standing dazed in the office whilst the computer slowly deleted all the systems that I'd set up for Si-Sidecars. I didn't need the job anyway and from now on I would be too busy concentrating on the two most important things in my life, my daughters and my new found business, Nice 'n Sleazy.

CHAPTER FORTY SIX

I'd e-mailed Antonio earlier on in the day and when I got home to an empty house I switched on my laptop and found that he had e-mailed me back. I hadn't heard from him in a while and I was happy that everything was working out well for him and Sinead. He loved his job and Sinead seemed happy enough with hers, even if it did involve travelling all over Ireland and the UK. I'd told him about the party but hadn't gone as far as telling him about Natalie's father or of her being pregnant.

I was kind of pissed off about what Jim had done to me in the office but in a way I was grateful as well. He was never a nice character in the first place and now that he wasn't doing as many of the tours as he used to he'd become really twisted and it was noticeable on his face when he returned from the pub, his usual pug-like ugly features even more contorted, as if in a state of perpetual anger. I guess I would have been angry at the world too if

I'd been a man and had been burdened with such a small excuse for a penis. In retrospect I was surprised he'd even had the balls or the dexterity for that matter, to get it out!

That little thing underneath that fat white belly; urgh, it doesn't bear thinking about.

I e-mailed Antonio back and told him about me quitting my job and he surprised me by phoning me only minutes after I'd sent him the mail.

"You need to take him for sexual harassment," Antonio said angrily.

"You couldn't take him for sexual harassment," I said laughing. "All he'd have to do if it got as far as court would be to take it out and any judge worth his salt would know that you couldn't harass anyone sexually with something so small."

Antonio still didn't see the funny side of it, but it was great to hear his voice again. I missed him terribly and wondered if he felt the same about me.

"Sinead is in London right now so I'm out partying every night," he joked. "It's supposed to be summer here but all it's done is piss down for the last three weeks. I miss the sun, you should see me, I don't even look Italian anymore, I'm so white. We're planning a trip to Mexico later, I've always wanted to go to Mexico. I love tequila and beans," he said in all seriousness.

Can anyone really love beans? I wondered.

When he put down the phone I felt less angry and more determined to make our business even more successful than it was. I Googled The Reflex in Corralejo and found their contact details, forgetting that I already had their telephone number on the poster that Susan and Bill had given me for my birthday. I tried ringing a couple of times but there was no answer so I fired off a quick e-mail outlining my proposal to host a Nice 'n Sleazy party at their club sometime next week. I then contacted our suppliers and placed an order for some more of the most popular items that Erika had highlighted in the suppliers catalogue. Before I knew it, it was almost dinner time and Natalie and Erika still hadn't returned home. I rang Natalie's number and just as I was about to put down the phone a breathless Natalie answered.

"Hi mum, we were just about to ring you. Erika and I are over at Bianca's house and we're going to stay the night if that's alright with you."

"Okay love, I wondered where you guys were. What's Bianca's house like?" I asked. I'd been told it was one of her ex husbands' houses and she'd been given it as part of the divorce settlement.

"You should see it mum, it's got a huge pool and would you believe it's even got its own wine cellar? It's just a pity I can't drink, you know, with me being pregnant and all."

I hadn't known about the wine cellar and I pondered the possibility that Bianca's ex husband could have been the man I'd spent the night with some time ago; Roger.

"What time will you be back tomorrow?"

"Probably late morning, you'll be working anyway, I'll see you when you finish work tomorrow."

I couldn't be bothered to explain what had happened to me at work over the phone so I said my goodbyes and hung up.

A night on my own at last; so what was it to be, the old faithful Rabbit or one of our more specialist vibrators?

I climbed into bed and fell into a deep sleep without even touching any of my new sex toy collection.

CHAPTER FORTY SEVEN

I woke early and drove down to the beach for a swim. Instead of going to the more popular beach I headed down to the pebbled beach between Las Salinas and Caleta which I knew to be a secluded area and swam naked. It had been such a long time since I'd been skinny dipping that I'd forgotten how liberating it could be. I vowed that now I wasn't working as such I would do it more often.

After returning home to a shower and breakfast I decided to call into some of the more reputable estate agents to find a new house for us. It was all well and good Natalie sleeping on the sofa for now but if she was staying with us permanently we were going to have to find a house with a separate bedroom for her and the baby. I called into three different agents before I found a house that would be within our budget and would meet all of our requirements. In fact the house I found would surpass all our requirements and, as it was situated at the far echelons of the newly built golf course, it should be fantastically quiet as well. I arranged to view the property by myself early the next day, feeling guilty that I hadn't even discussed Natalie staying with us on a permanent basis with Erika.

I drove up the hill excited by the prospect of a potential move. Unlike most people, I loved moving house and all the excitement that came with discovering new things both within the house and within the neighbourhood.

"Shit," exclaimed Natalie, as I opened the front door to find her lying naked underneath an equally naked Erika, her face jammed between Natalie's legs.

"What the...?" I screamed as both girls scrambled to snatch up the duvet spread out underneath them.

I slammed Erika's bedroom door shut and stomped downstairs to the lounge. My heart was thumping and my hands were shaking. I tried to pour myself a glass of water but ended up spilling most of it on the kitchen counter.

My daughter isn't a lesbian, she's pregnant for God's sake; this is all Erika's doing, she's tainted her, brainwashed her or something.

I could hear them shuffling around upstairs and I hoped that they wouldn't come down for a while, I needed time to think. I was angry, angry that Erika could use my little girl for her own selfish gratification, angry that I'd trusted her and she'd abused her position of trust, angry with Natalie for, well, I didn't really know why I was angry at her, perhaps for letting Erika use her, but I was furious nevertheless. There are just some lines that you don't cross and as far as I was concerned Erika had just crossed that line. And Natalie, what was she playing at, she's got a baby on the way?

I tried gathering my thoughts as I heard them splashing about in the bathroom obviously cleaning up after their sordid...*Oh God, I can't handle this!* On one hand my mind was telling me that Natalie was an adult, old enough to make her own choices and decisions and on the other hand Natalie was still my baby, my first born and Erika was no better than a rapist, taking advantage of her youth and her hormonal vulnerability, everyone knows that your hormones are all over the place when you're pregnant.

In the space of twenty four hours I'd lost my job, my trust in my business partner, flatmate and best friend and if I didn't handle this with kid gloves, perhaps my daughter as well. The urge to simply pack a suitcase and flee was overwhelming but I couldn't go through life running away from everything, I'd already done that when I moved over here, and it was only yesterday I'd vowed to become a better mother to my daughters. I knew that the way I dealt with this situation would have a huge impact on my future and, when I heard the patter of bare feet approaching down the stairs, my heart was in my mouth.

Both of them looked nervous and frightened as they sat side by side on the couch facing me, their faces pinched white. This threw me completely as I was so used to seeing Erika oozing confidence. Their eyes however still bore the twinkle of their passion that first time lovers get that no amount of fear could extinguish, and this made me angry and envious of their togetherness at the same time. I knew I was alone in this battle.

"When?" I asked.

"Last night was the first time," answered Natalie, a tone of defiance in her voice.

"And you thought that it was acceptable to fuck my daughter did you?" I asked Erika as she squirmed into the couch as if she hoped that it would swallow her up.

"She didn't fuck me mum; we made love - there is a difference."

"Make love, fuck, it's all the same to me, anyway I wasn't asking you, I was talking to her."

Erika shrugged, "We get on well, it just happened."

"Get on well, what sort of excuse is that, I get on well with all sorts of people but I'm not ripping their clothes off and shagging them in their own mother's house at every available opportunity?" I answered hysterically.

"Mum, stop it now," said Natalie starting to cry. "Erika and I, we like each other a lot, what's so bad about that? I'm sorry that you walked in on us, we thought you'd be at work. We didn't set out to hurt you and let me ask you this; if you'd have come home and found me with a man would you have reacted in the same way? I think not... I'd like you to be happy for us," she said taking Erika's hand in hers in defiance.

"Your best friend and your daughter are lovers, so what; there are much worse things than that. I'm twenty two years old, I'm not a child anymore and I don't need your approval of who I choose to sleep with."

"Exactly; you're twenty two years old, Erika is thirty five, almost the same age as me. Why would you want a relationship with someone as old as your mother?"

"Come on mum you know that's bullshit, look at you

and Antonio, how old was he, twenty four or something like that?"

"Yeah okay but that's different. Anyway he was twenty five."

"Different how, because he's a man? I know why you're upset and it's because I'm with a woman. Well let me tell you a little secret mum, it's not the first time I've been with a woman so don't go thinking that Erika's to blame here, I was the one who instigated everything. I knew from the moment I saw her dancing in the rain that I wanted her. Even if she had been your neighbour or just someone visiting I would have found her; I know most people don't believe in love at first sight or all that soul-mate crap but that's what I felt as soon as I saw her. All those years you convinced yourself that Natalie was the innocent one, it's Angie that you had got to worry about; that left the coast clear for me to do exactly what I wanted so while you two were watching Angie like a hawk, behind your back I was fucking half the neighbourhood."

Blinking back tears I felt dizzy. Natalie scowled at me defiantly.

"Mum, I'm a young woman," she said softly, "I enjoy sex. Male, female, hell, even one of your vibrators does it for me. It doesn't make me abnormal and the truth is I trust Erika more than almost anyone else that I've had sex with before. There's a connection there and I think it might even be love and I know without a shadow of a doubt that Erika feels the same way about me. I know you feel hurt and upset and even cheated by the relationship that we have but we've made a decision that we are going to make a go of what it is we have going with or without your approval." She leaned across Erika and kissed her lovingly

I sat frozen in the chair.

My daughter a slut, a whore, fucking half of the neighbourhood; How could I not have known? What sort of mother was I? But she's my daughter and I love her and I love Erika too, she's the best friend I've ever had and neither of them are bad people, in fact they're lovely people, people I want in my life, people I need in my life. Natalie and Angie are my reason for living and Erika, well she's a big part of my life too. Why am I so angry?

I'd never felt so confused in my life. I mean what harm were they doing really? It's just sex really, women having sex with women was socially acceptable nowadays and more or less compulsory in Hollywood films. No wonder girls grow up so confused nowadays. The only problem that I could see arising would be the day Erika dumped her for someone else which I was sure would happen. If not before she'd given birth then at least afterwards when she suddenly realised that her partner was a single, exhausted mum who spent her days changing nappies and hanging around the house in baggy tracksuits, sans make-up or exotic lingerie. Also, now that I discovered that I didn't really know Natalie as well as I'd thought I had, I wasn't sure how strong she really was as a person. Would she be able to face the world and their snide comments when she came out as openly gay or would she...

"Come on mum, say something, anything. I've poured my heart out to you and this is hurting Erika and me more than you realise. I love you mum, both of us love you and this is just needlessly tearing us apart." Natalie said, interrupting my confused thoughts.

I could feel the trickle of tears making their way slowly down my face.

"Dad doesn't want me, well not dad but you know what I mean, the dickhead who knocked me up doesn't want me and it would break my heart to lose you too. All I want, all we want is acceptance. If you can grant us that then I promise you right here, right now, that we won't throw it in your face. We'll be very discreet and you'll hardly even know that we're a couple. Both of us just want things to get back to the way it was, don't we babe?"

God she just called Erika babe! I don't know if I can do this; there's no mother's manual available out there to teach you how to deal with situations like this.

"Okay," I whispered.

"Okay what mum?"

"Okay I accept that you're a couple."

Natalie stood up and pulling Erika up by her hand they approached my chair and bending down they both hugged me tightly as all three of us cried together; mother, daughter, best friend, lover...

CHAPTER FORTY EIGHT

Everything got back to normal, well as normal as things could be when your daughter and your best girlfriend were sharing a bed in your house with your approval but, by the end of the week, it all seemed sort of worthwhile as Natalie was happier than I'd ever seen her before and for this I was grateful. Even Erika had stopped tip toeing around me and seemed to be back to her old self. Now that Erika and Natalie had made a commitment together it was obvious that Natalie had no intention of returning to the UK so, after I viewed the house on the new golf course the morning after our tiff and felt that it met with my approval, I told the other two about it and they were eager to move in without even bothering to see it.

Whilst I was walking down the high street to hand in my notice on the old place I bumped into one of the two Steves and asked him if he knew anything about Angie's boyfriend Aziz.

"'ere luv, it's not in my place to say but your Angie's 'angin' out wiv a rite bad lot."

"What do you mean bad lot?" I asked thinking that if Steve thought that they were bad then they must be terrible.

"Well luv, your Angie isn't wot, sixteen or summat? I've 'erd about all sorts of goings on in that there villa of theirs. Drugs, orgies...the lot, 'av' even seen a bit of the ol' dirty stuff goin´ on at that 'ouse on't internet. I'd get 'er out if I was you, that Aziz is a rite dirty cunt of a Moroccan."

Drugs...Orgies, on the internet; if Aziz has hurt my daughter I'll have him castrated.

"You're sure it's the same house Steve, the one Rachael and Angie live in?"

He nodded his head.

"And my Angie or Rachael, are they in any of these videos?"

"Look luv, I ain't gettin' involved, ah only said summat ´cos she's only a kid like, just get her out yeah."

"I will do Steve...Thanks."

Things just seem to go from bad to worse. At least by us taking the new house there would be room for Angie to stay as well. I just didn't know how easy it would be to get her out, it's not like we're not on friendly terms or anything but I know that Angie won't want her freedom taken away from her and it would definitely cause a big rift between us but it's for her own good and regardless of the consequences to our relationship she would be leaving that house today.

After handing in my notice I drove straight home, hoping that Erika and Natalie would be there. I needed them for moral and perhaps physical support.

Erika threatened to beat Aziz to death with one of our Big Boy dildos but I managed to convince her that she would look ridiculous threatening someone with a fifteen inch dildo although she did have a point, we could always overpower him and tie him up and shove all fifteen inches right up his ass. We drove over to the house, its bland façade hiding a multitude of sordid secrets. Rachael came to the gate when we rang the bell. She too had a huge black eye. She baulked when she saw that it was me.

"What's going on in this house Rachael?" I asked pushing her aside, striding down the narrow path purposefully.

Rachael followed behind me constantly repeating that Angie wasn't in. Natalie told her in no uncertain terms to shut up which she sensibly did straight away. Pushing my way through the patio doors I was amazed at what a mess the house was in. The kitchen to the left was piled with what looked like hundreds of dirty dishes and the majority of them were blackened with thousands of buzzing flies. The youngest of the kids was crawling shirtless on a dirty rug in the lounge, shit leaking out of the sides of his nappy, down his legs and leaving a stinking trail behind him. Video games, DVD´s and magazines littered the lounge floor. I couldn't believe that one of my daughters lived here.

I turned and grabbed Rachael by her shoulders.

"Where is she, where's Angie?"

"She's through there," admitted Rachael, indicating a closed door just inside the corridor.

I rushed forward and pulled the door open expecting

the worst, but found Angie sat at a dressing table in her underwear applying her make-up.

"Hi mum, what brings you here?" she asked, smiling as if I was here under perfectly normal circumstances.

Her room was surprisingly tidy after the rubbish tip that we'd just walked through.

"I'm taking you home," I said hugging her skinny frame, her ribs all sticking out like a starving Ethiopian.

"Okay," she said unsurprised, the fearsome fight that was her constant companion seemed to have just evaporated into the stale and fetid air inside the house.

What had they done to my baby girl?

"She's high as a kite," said Erika, "I'm surprised she even knows who you are."

"Where's Aziz?" I asked Angie, but she just smiled at her reflection as if I wasn't there.

Erika and Natalie packed her suitcase and I helped her get dressed. On the way to the car I dialled 112 and reported that there was a house on the golf course where lots of under-age people were drinking alcohol, having sex and taking drugs. I explained that they had a baby within their charge as well, knowing that it would kick them into action immediately. As soon as I told them that their ringleader was a Moroccan around eighteen years old called Aziz the police informed me that they knew exactly who he was and as he was in Fuerteventura illegally they assured me that as soon as they managed to locate him he would be put into detention until he could be deported.

I liked the Spanish police, they didn't pussyfoot around.

Angie sat in the car besides her sister smiling

beatifically. I had no idea what drug or combination of drugs she had taken but they didn't seem to harm her at all, in fact, she seemed to be perfectly complacent. I could do with a shed load of whatever she'd taken for when she came down off of the stuff for I knew she would be angry. Natalie stroked at her hair and traced the faded home-made tattoo on the back of Angle's hand. I'd never seen them so close and after Natalie's revelations I wondered just how many secrets the two of them shared.

It would be good to have both my daughters at home with me regardless of how damaged they may appear and I hoped that their togetherness would make them stronger in much the same way that Natalie's relationship with Erika had make her bloom. Finally we would be a family again; a slightly screwed up, non-convention sort of family but a family nevertheless and that felt great; it wasn't just Vanessa versus the world anymore.

CHAPTER FORTY NINE

When Angie discovered that she'd been permanently removed from the den of iniquity that she'd called home all hell broke loose. She smashed a few things in the kitchen and threw the microwave through the window. Instead of punishing her I hugged her tightly and told her how much I loved her until the fire just went out of her.

I explained to her that the house had been raided by the police and even if she had wanted to go back she wouldn't have been able to. The two young kids had been taken into a foster home and Rachael had been lucky enough to be allowed to go back home to her mother. The owners of the house had been arrested and charged for employment of a minor and allowing illegal activities to take place in their place of residence. The house had been fire-bombed two nights after I'd removed Angie from the premises and all that remained were a few blackened concrete blocks and the outside wall and gate which now bore the legend paedophile in big red spray-painted letters. Aziz was still on the run but I was assured by the police that he would be found soon.

Fuerteventura was too small a place to hide.

I began feeding Angie up, trying to get her back to a reasonable weight but for the first three days anything she ate seemed to come back up. It was like living in a home for bulimics, what with Natalie's morning sickness and Angie's regurgitation of her food and I was really pleased once Angie started keeping down her meals. I drove down to the secluded beach in the morning with Angie at my side and on the third day she joined me in the water. Slowly our fragile bond was returning and I was surprised when we drove home that morning when Angie complained how hungry she was.

We never spoke about any of the goings on in the house and Angie didn't volunteer any information, but as far as I was concerned whatever had happened there was in the past and the future we were tentatively building together right now was of far greater importance.

In the meantime Erika had managed to host two private parties that yielded us yet again an impressive amount of cash. Bianca had one to do this week and I was at present making plans for our *pièce de résistance,* the massive party we planned to host in Corralejo at The Reflex. If everything went according to plan we could expect up to five hundred plus women and we would have to employ extra hosts to maintain control of the event. Rather than having a convention sex toy promotion party we were planning a whole host of events including male strippers and one of the most outrageous competitions so far, the giant butt-plug competition. It would certainly not be a night for the faint hearted, I'd seen how a hundred and eighty rowdy women could behave but over five hundred; I was worried that we would end up having to call the fire brigade in to hose them down.

I spoke with Erika and Natalie about allowing Angie to act as a host on the big night but both girls were concerned about the police raiding the club and finding us having an under-age girl working for us, even if she was my daughter, and I conceded that they had a valid point. I knew that we had to involve Angie in everything that we did just to maintain her interest or else we would lose the tentative hold that we had on her. I used to believe that Angie was the stronger of my two girls but I was quickly learning how insecure and weak and completely dependent on other people she actually was.

I noticed that since she had moved in with us she had begun replacing several of her facial piercings and rather than frown upon it I actively encouraged her by buying her a few new pieces and then taking her down to Pete's Tattoo Shop in Caleta to get her home-made tattoos covered with one's that at least didn't look as though they'd been inscribed in a jail cell. Whilst we were there Angie asked why I didn't have any tattoos and after a brief discussion it was decided that Angie and I would have a tattoo each on our upper thigh. We chose quite a big abstract design and asked Pete if he could make it look like it had been torn in half to enable Angie to have one half of the tattoo and me to have the other half, which he did quite happily. Once

Pete had finished with the two of us he took a photo of us stood together, our skirts raised and our legs touching. It looked great and both Angie and I loved it and I asked him to print off another copy for me to keep. I felt closer to Angie than I had in a long time and our joint tattoo helped cement our rediscovered bond better than any spoken words or big promises.

I hope to God that Angie doesn't expect me to be piercing my cheeks next.

CHAPTER FIFTY

Karen, the lady from the estate agency phoned me on my mobile later in the day and informed me that if I wished to have the keys for the new house earlier it wouldn't be a problem and that if I was passing their office I could pick them up. I drove down the hill, all four of us in my little car, excited by the prospect of our move. At least once we had the keys we could start moving things in little by little rather than attempting to do it all in one day in a mad rush.

It was a beautiful clear day and it complemented my mood perfectly. Psychologically as soon as everything starts going right for me I begin to worry that something is lurking around the corner determined to upend everything. This results in my moments of happiness becoming toned down by a cautious pessimism. Today however everything felt perfect and as I glanced at Angie alongside me and Erika and Natalie in my rear view mirror I was elated just to live in that moment. I knew in times of sadness I would recall this very memory to remind me of how great my life had been.

The house was still dusty from the builders and had that overpowering unlived in smell but beyond that you could see the potential of a great home just in the sheer size of the place. Angie bounced up and down like a child on the bed in her chosen bedroom and Natalie and Erika were chuffed with their bedroom, which was right at the far end of the house where they could maintain their privacy whilst also having their own en suite bathroom.

The furniture was all new and still covered in plastic but you could tell that the owner had chosen to use quality furniture rather than the cheap Spanish stuff that most other landlords favoured. I chose the smallest bedroom as I wasn't really a person who carried much physical baggage and all I needed in my room really was a bed and a small desk where I could write. Oh, and cupboard space for my shoes. I have a weakness for shoes.

Outside there was a nine by five metre swimming pool which was covered at the moment but which I could see us all using most of the year round and to the side of the pool there was a double enclosed garage which we could use as a warehouse for our ever increasing stock. We were picking up new product almost every week nowadays and the customs guys nowadays referred to me as the sexy lady. I planned to run an ADSL line into the garage and I hoped that we could use the space to prepare and package all of our online purchases from there. I wanted Angie to handle our online sales but I would have to get her up to speed on the computer; Angie was the most computer illiterate teenager I'd ever met. Who knows maybe I could even teach her how to set up a Facebook page?

The house was perfect and as I set about rearranging my room to my liking, I had an epiphany at that very moment that my ultimate aim was to one day purchase the same type of house for myself in the future. It had been a while since I had thought about any sort of long term plans and simply thinking about buying a house on the island was a huge commitment yet, rather than frightening me, it gave me a goal, something to aim for, somewhere where I could build a lasting legacy, spend time and create memories along with the two most important people in my life, Natalie and Angie.

The phone rang startling me out of my real estate fantasy. It was Paco, the owner of The Reflex. We arranged everything for the first Saturday of next month. Hiring the club was going to cost us around eight hundred euros plus we had the cost of the strippers, the promotional advertising and the extra staff. On the plus side our suppliers had started giving us a very favourable discount due to the high volume of stock that we'd been purchasing from them but even so we had a lot riding on this night and, although I was excited about the mother of all parties that we were planning to host, I was also very wary of all the things that could go wrong.

What if we didn't reach our sales targets? What if a meteorite struck the venue just before opening night? Stop being ridiculous Vanessa!

CHAPTER FIFTY ONE

We managed to be completely moved into the new house three days before the end of the month, which also happened to be Erika's birthday. I bought both her and Natalie a full day at the spa and the receptionist who sold me the tickets threw in two chocolate wraps for free. I knew Erika loved chocolate and I would have to remind her not to try eating the stuff off of herself or off Natalie for that matter, as they were putting it on. It would be nice for them to have some quality time by themselves. All we seemed to be doing over the last few days had been packing and unpacking, if it wasn't furniture or personal possessions it was sex toys, and although Natalie hadn't been doing much of the heavy lifting, Erika had always been around to help, often leaving Natalie by herself.

The telephone company surprised me by turning up on time to install our internet and, on the day that Natalie and Erika went to the spa, I coaxed a reluctant Angie into our garage cum warehouse for a spot of computer training. She knew how to use a mouse but had absolutely no idea how to send or read e-mails or even how to browse the web. She thrilled me by how quickly she mastered everything and by how articulate she could be when she wanted to be and after just an hour and a half I felt confident that she would be able to handle the day to day affairs of online purchasing for N & S. I left her attempting to contact some of her old friends back in the UK on her newly created Facebook page.

My mobile phone began ringing just as I stepped inside and I was surprised to see that it was Antonio.

"Hey Antonio, how are you?" I asked.

"Hey Vanessa," answered Antonio, his voice cracking. "I'm phoning to tell you that Sinead is in hospital," he began to cry. "They're not sure if she will make it," he sniffed loudly and I heard him curse under his breath.

"My God Antonio, what happened?"

"Fucking taxi driver hit her last night, she's in intensive care in England, I've just got back from seeing her. She don't look good."

What have the doctor's said?"

"She has a ruptured spleen, a few crushed, how you say, vertibri?"

"Yes vertebrae."

"A few crushed vertebrae, both her hips are crushed. He drove straight up the pavement and rammed her against a wall."

I could hear his voice quivering as he spoke and I realised that I was crying too.

"Who are you with?" I asked.

"Just Sinead's mother is here, it's just me and her."

"Where's your closest airport?" I asked.

"I don't understand."

"The closest airport; which airport did you fly into from Ireland?"

"I flew into Gatwick."

"Okay Antonio, I'm booking myself a flight to Gatwick for as soon as I can, I'll ring you as soon as I get to London, I'm not having you going through this yourself, okay."

"Okay Vanessa, you are a good friend. Thank you."

"No problem Antonio, you take care now and I'll see you soon."

"Okay, bye."

"Bye."

I put down the phone and immediately dialled Debbie, a girl I knew who worked at one of the budget travel agencies on the island and within fifteen minutes I'd secured a one way flight into Gatwick for seven o'clock that evening. I knew that Erika and my two girls would understand, I couldn't leave a friend in need in a foreign place all on their own.

I whispered an almost silent prayer under my breath for Sinead.

CHAPTER FIFTY TWO

Erika drove me over to the airport in my car, freshly spruced from her day at the spa. I was excited to be leaving the island even if it was for the wrong reasons but I was still concerned about Angie's welfare. Erika assured me that both her and Natalie would make sure that they were with her at all times, except of course on the big night at The Reflex. I couldn't believe that I stood a huge chance of not being in Fuerteventura on what was to be our big night, but my friend's well-being took priority over financial gain and I knew that Erika would find somebody as good as, or perhaps even better than I would be, as a host.

The flight was the usual uneventful noisy affair with last minute sunburned tourists drinking as much as they could from the trolley service and everybody under the age of three crying consistently. They really needed to introduce a first or business class rather than throwing everybody into economy and expecting them to be happy and to get along with everybody. I slipped my earphones on and tried to ignore the constant interruptions of the air hostesses attempting to sell me extortionately priced miniature boxes of Pringles and Toblerones that required hand baggage just to get them off the plane.

We disembarked into a light grey drizzle, the raindrops amplified in size by the bright orange sodium lamps lighting up the demarcated areas alongside the runway. A fine fog was descending from behind the airport terminus and what struck me most of all was that the air smelled different, not unpleasant or polluted but it had a sort of weirdness that you could almost taste, not dissimilar to the taste of sticking the positive terminal of a battery onto the end of your tongue.

I followed the crowds towards the baggage carousel, my feet feeling slightly swollen in my ballerina flats, the four Toblerones I'd been convinced to buy in flight making it appear as though someone had smuggled a hefty house brick into my handbag when I wasn't looking. Typically my suitcase was the last to make its way through the hatch above the carousel and by the time I made my way into the arrivals hall it was more or less deserted.

After locating a call box I dropped a pound coin into the telephone and rang Antonio to tell him I'd arrived. I asked if it would be best if I rented a car but he recommended I catch a cab over to Dorking to the Bridge House Hotel which was where he was staying as it was only about a twenty minute ride in the evening when the roads were quieter. They'd been catching the bus over to the hospital as it was the cheapest way of getting around and it didn't take me long to understand why he'd taken finances into consideration. I'd forgotten how expensive everything was over here and was jolted into remembering when I happened to notice the price of cigarettes. I was grateful I'd given up the habit.

The Asian taxi driver asked me where I was going and once he'd set off didn't attempt to speak to me for the rest of the journey. I watched the traffic and the brightly lit houses and shops interspersed with lonely dark spaces. For such a populated country England sure seemed to have a lot of open space.

I handed over the thirty two pound fare, reluctantly leaving the driver a three pound tip, and hoped that I had brought enough money along with me. Entering the hotel I asked the receptionist if she could call Antonio and let him know that I was here. I barely recognised him as he stepped into the foyer. His dark hair was now grey at the temples and his skin was whiter than I'd ever imagined was possible. He'd also lost weight, not in a good way, and I was reminded of how Angie was when we'd pulled her from the house on the golf course. He offered me a strained smile.

"Vanessa...so good to see you," he said stepping into my open arms.

I could feel his ribs digging into me as he hugged me tightly.

"You look good," he said pulling back from me and running his chocolate eyes over me in appraisal.

"You don't look so good Antonio, how are you holding up?"

"You know, things are bad. Sinead's mother she cries all

the time and that makes me cry. I'm trying to be strong but it's not easy; there's no change in her condition and even if by some miracle she was to come round, the doctors they say she will never walk again. At the moment she is on a machine to keep her alive and there's no active activity in the brain which is very bad. They say…" Antonio wiped at his eyes.

"They say it would be better to switch off the machine but it is not up to me, it is up to Sinead's mother and she doesn't want to give up hope just yet."

I longed to tell him that it would be alright but I knew that this was something way beyond my resolve and that all I could offer was moral support. I leaned back into Antonio and held him tight until I could feel that he was recovered from having to describe the horrendous details of his constant nightmare to me. When we parted I asked what the accommodation arrangements were and was surprised to find that I would be staying with Antonio in his room. The hotel had been very good to both Antonio and Sinead's mother and when Antonio had explained that a friend was coming over from overseas to be with him they had arranged for him to change rooms at no extra cost so that he could have twin single beds rather than the traditional double.

"You don't mind do you?" he asked sheepishly, "I should have asked you first."

"No that's great, I was willing to take a room of my own, but it'll be even better if we're sharing."

"Are you hungry at all? I can order up room service if you want."

"No thanks love, I already ate on the plane, I just fancy a really good coffee like a Starbucks or something."

"There's a coffee shop around the corner, Costa Coffee or something like that, we'll drop your suitcase off and pop back down and you can get a coffee."

Shit I'd forgotten Antonio only drank coffee in the morning or after sex.

The room was sparsely furnished but clean with just the twin beds, a small desk and an old fashioned portable television. I couldn't imagine spending a lot of time in there.

We dropped off my suitcase and I removed the huge chocolates from my handbag. I swear I heard my handbag's straps groan a sigh of relief.

"Toblerone?" asked Antonio quizzically, "I thought you'd more or less given up on chocolate."

"I have," I answered, "This one's for you and the other three are for Angie and Natalie and Natalie's girlfriend Erika."

I'd told Antonio about Erika being my housemate but tonight was the first time I'd referred to her as Natalie's girlfriend. I'd expected that when I told people about my daughter having a girlfriend I'd feel uncomfortable or embarrassed and that I would have to explain myself further but Antonio didn't pick up on it at all and I wasn't going to burden him with any of my own trials and tribulations unless he asked me. Besides I realised that I had become quite accustomed to the fact that Natalie was in a lesbian relationship and that I didn't care at all what others may think.

We headed downstairs and I ordered the biggest strong

black coffee imaginable with absolutely no thought to the insomnia I may have burdened myself with and, as I carefully steered our conversation away from that of the present and back to the old times, it was as if time had stood still and I could see the tension around Antonio's eyes and jaw-line began to soften the more we spoke. The transformation was clearly visible and it was great seeing him starting to loosen up a little. I hoped that our reminiscing, this little break from his unfortunate reality, would do him a world of good. I know it did me: I'd missed Antonio oh so much more than I would have liked to admit.

CHAPTER FIFTY THREE

I awoke the next morning to the sound of Antonio in the shower. Picking up my mobile phone from the floor next to my bed I dialled home.

"Nice 'n Sleazy online retailers, how may I help you?" said Angie in a substantially posh voice that I wouldn't usually recognise. I'd forgotten that we were going to use the landline number purely for the business and continue using our mobiles for private conversations.

"Angie love, it's me,"

"Oh, hiya mum. What's England like?" answered Angie reverting to her normal way of speaking.

"I'm not sure yet, I'm still in bed; you sounded a bit posh answering the phone like that."

I pictured her blushing as I paid her the complement and I felt myself missing my girls more than ever.

"I don't want to talk too long 'cos I'm on my Spanish mobile and you know I'm going to have to take a loan from the bank to pay my phone bill if I chatter away. I just wanted to let you know that I've arrived okay and that if you can't get hold of me on my mobile I'm staying at The Bridge House Hotel in Dorking, you'll have to ask for Mr. Minnelli's room."

"Mum, you're not staying in his room are you?"

"I am love but it's not like you're thinking, we've got separate beds and everything," I explained wondering why I had to justify my living arrangements to my youngest daughter. "I'm going now, love and kisses to Natalie and Erika and I'll see you guys soon, take care love; I love you lots."

"Bye mum," said Angie. I let the dial tone ring on for about twenty seconds before I disconnected the call.

Antonio stepped into the room with a towel around his waist, his emaciated ribs sticking out like a skeleton.

"God Antonio, I'm taking you out for a huge meal tonight, I've never seen you so skinny."

"I know Vanessa but it's pointless. I can't put the weight on, believe me I've tried. I guess it's time for me to tell you the truth, you'd find out soon enough anyway."

"What are you talking about...the truth?"

"The first month that I came to Ireland I started having problems with, you know, the piss. It didn't hurt much but I just couldn't piss, sometimes I would only piss once the whole day, it didn't matter how much I'd drunk. Sinead insisted I go and see a doctor but hey you know me, I'll put off going to see a doctor until maybe I'm dying but anyway Sinead books me an appointment with this old Irish doctor and she comes with me to make sure that I go. The first thing the doctor does is pull on a rubber glove and sticks his finger right up my ass." Antonio began laughing.

"I asked Sinead if all the doctors in Ireland do that as soon as you walk through their doors but apparently they don't. Anyway I did loads of tests, blood tests, piss tests, they took me forever, and they even x-rayed my bollocks. It turns out I've got cancer of the prostrate..."

I felt my breath stop.

"It's not as bad as it sounds and we caught it real early so there's a good chance that it's curable but the pills that I'm on at the moment," he stepped towards the desk drawer and removing a plastic packet he emptied the contents onto the desk. "I take eight of these a day, four of these and two of these," he said indicating all the different tablets. "I'm on like a clinical trial and although the pills seem to be reducing the cancer cells, they stop me from being hungry. Ever since I started taking them I started losing weight and I force myself to eat but I just get skinnier and skinnier. I could sell these pills to some of the fat girls in Ireland, there are loads of them, and make myself a small fortune I reckon." He smiled ruefully.

I couldn't believe what Antonio was going through. Not only was his fiancée likely to die but he also had his own serious health issues to deal with.

He must have pissed God off in another life!

For once I was speechless.

"We were going to tell everyone once I'd fully recovered. We'd planned to book the Mexico tickets for the time when my treatment was over so that whatever the results were I could go and pig out on tequila and beans."

He smiled at the thought of tequila and beans.

"Come on Vanessa, don't look so sad, I need you to be strong for me because I'm not sure if I'm strong enough for the both of us and when Sinead dies, which I know she is going to regardless of what people say, I'm going to need you to be my rock. I have no one else here besides you and I won't make it through all of this on my own. You being here for me right now is so important."

I had a quick shower and dressed in the confines of the small bathroom before meeting up with Sinead's mum downstairs. After brief introductions we visited a nearby café on the high street for some breakfast before heading over to the hospital. Sinead's mother seemed very dubious of the relationship between the two of us but didn't seem to dwell on it for too much time, obviously she had more pressing issues on her mind. Sinead's dad was flying over to join her the day after tomorrow and it would be then that a joint decision would be made as to what to do about Sinead's medical condition. The doctors were convinced that the lack of activity in the brain would have caused her serious irreparable brain damage and by keeping her alive on the machines they were only prolonging the inevitable.

As much as Antonio loved Sinead, I felt that if it were up to him he would have already allowed the machines keeping Sinead alive to be switched off. I hoped that if by any misfortune I happened to land myself in the same situation as her that my family would do the same thing. I'm not a deeply religious person but I do believe that we possess a soul and I would hate the thought of me floating around in limbo waiting for my final release.

I did, however, as a mother understand the dilemma that Sinead's mum was going through. I would do anything to maintain my children's survival and if I believed for just one second that there was a chance, no matter how mathematically small it was that my own daughter could pull through something as awful as this, I would latch onto it like a limpet and you'd be very hard pushed to make me let go.

Antonio ordered just a coffee with which to wash a couple of his tablets down but, even though I'm not much of a meat lover nowadays, I went for a full English as I was ravenous. I forced Antonio to eat half a slice of toast and a rasher of bacon from my plate which he did unenthusiastically, but without resistance. Sinead's mum ate her breakfast muffin quietly and methodically as if she was permanently distracted. I tried to make some sort of conversation with her but I soon grew tired of her one word answers or grunts and came to the conclusion that it was easier just to eat in relative silence, allowing the drone of Radio 2 piping throughout the café to mask the awkwardness at our table.

It was the first time I'd caught a bus in around eight years and I was quite excited by the prospect. I'd insisted that I sat upstairs much to the annoyance of Sinead's mum but the truth was, I was happy to get away from her. Don't get me wrong, I did feel sorry for her but that didn't really mean that I had to like her as far as I was concerned. I was sure she believed that I'd already begun jumping Antonio's bones before her daughter was dead and buried in her grave and I disliked her even more for thinking that I would do such a thing.

"Does she know you're sick?" I asked once we'd settled into the front seats on the top deck of the bus.

"Like I said to you we didn't really want to tell anybody until we were aware of the final results of the drug trial. Look, I know she can be a bit of a bitch, but put yourself in her shoes and you'd probably behave in the same manner. She's also probably jealous that she's here alone and that I have someone to help me get through, at least Sinead's dad will be here in a couple of days and I'm sure she'll become a little bit nicer then."

The bus jerked and rattled its way through the morning traffic and it wasn't long before we'd reached our destination.

Entering the hospital I followed behind the two of them as they made their way with the confidence of frequent visitors towards the ICU. Once we were there I was shown to a seat and told to wait. Only family and relatives were allowed to visit and to be honest I was quite grateful, I'd rather remember Sinead the way that she was rather than the way that she is now.

I watched efficient yet harried doctors and nurses rushing around the hospital in a blur of white coats. It was peaceful enough in this ward though compared to the traumatic chaos we'd ploughed through downstairs. I had a healthy respect for the people who dedicated their lives to others in the dark underbelly of poorly funded hospitals but I had created a deep seated irrational fear of the places for myself since my dad had passed away.

I knew that I had to be strong for Antonio so I smiled

encouragingly at him as he vacated the small reception room and headed over to where Sinead was all wired up. The receptionist asked me whether I would like a coffee whilst I waited which I refused politely, recalling how bad the coffee had been when my dad had been in hospital. I was surprised that the hospital was as clean as it was. The hospital that my dad was in before he died had smelled permanently of urine and you didn't have enough fingers and toes to count the number of cobwebs that trailed across the yellowing ceilings.

I flipped through a well thumbed, three year old copy of Home & Garden and wondered how things were back in Fuerteventura. I'd only really been away for a day but I was already missing my family.

Antonio and I had made plans for me to head over to my publishers to meet with Tessa, my agent, once we were finished in the hospital and I thought that it would be a good break from his routine to get out a little and perhaps to get away from Sinead's mum for a while; sitting in your hotel room whilst you waited for your fiancée to die probably wasn't the best way to deal with his situation. Antonio had never been to London before and although it was obvious that he wasn't here to see the sights, it would be nice for him just to see the usual things that would be on any tourists list; Big Ben, The Houses of Parliament, Tower Bridge, The London Eye...

Perhaps I was being harsh by forcing him to come along with me, perhaps I could ruin the sight of those landmarks for him for the rest of his life, but I was only doing what I thought was best for him. I hadn't even thought to ask him whether his cancer made it difficult for him to walk but I hadn't noticed any difference to his usual gait so I assumed that it wouldn't be a problem. The thing I hoped most to achieve on this day would be just to get a glimpse of his old wicked smile that he was so fond of sharing before all of this happened.

When the two of them emerged from the ICU in floods of tears I had to swallow hard to stop myself from joining them.

Come on Vanessa; you've got to be strong.

CHAPTER FIFTY FOUR

We took the overground train from Dorking to Waterloo and then changed over to the tube. Unlike the excitement I'd felt catching the bus for the first time in years, the prospect of using the underground daunted me. I envied the way residents could just settle back into their seats (if they were lucky enough to actually claim a seat) and get off of the train without having even taken their eyes from their books or newspapers. I spent the entire journey studying the colourful lines on the map next to an advertisement for teeth whitening, just below the carriage's roof. Every time the train stopped I ducked down and frantically scanned the platform for the sign to let me know that we were still on the right network and that we hadn't missed our stop.

Antonio was silent throughout the journey although conversations on the tube were difficult enough at the best of times with all the deafening clatter that they made; in fact I'm sure that regular tube users would most certainly require hearing aids after several years of tube travel.

I was starting to feel a little shell shocked by the time we reached our stop, unused to the sheer volume of people and the endless frantic rush that caused everybody to run around as if possessed by tireless demons.

Wouldn't it be a great thing if everybody in London just stopped what they were doing all at once, even for just a few seconds so that some of them could experience silence for the first time in their lives?

We disembarked at our station and took the steep escalator upwards towards vaguely fresher air, standing to one side as everyone pushed past us. It felt strange not to be in any sort of hurry and I found I had to pull myself back from picking up the same breakneck speed as the other pedestrians as we trudged the litter strewn pavement, trying to find Africa House where my publishers were located.

Tessa was really nice, it was the first time we'd met face to face, and she was quite happy to allow Antonio to sit in with us as she discussed the various menial tasks that not only the publishers, but me as well would have to undertake to ensure a smooth release of my book come December. As soon as we'd finished we set off on the tourist trail and ended the day on the London Eye. I had managed to take several photos of Antonio on my phone but not one of them showed his real smile and although I kept the day as light-hearted as I possibly could I was beginning to worry that Antonio would never get back to becoming the carefree happy spirited person I knew and loved. We returned to the hospital for the late afternoon visit where I shed a silent tear for the loss of not only Sinead but of Antonio as well. I knew there wasn't a thing I could do about Sinead but I vowed to get the old Antonio back regardless of whatever was needed for me to do so.

CHAPTER FIFTY FIVE

The day that Sinead's dad arrived in Dorking was the day of the huge Nice 'n Sleazy party at The Reflex. Using one of those confusing international phone cards I phoned Fuerteventura that morning whilst Antonio and Sinead's parents visited Sinead in hospital. I spoke to both Natalie and Angie about general things; it was great to hear their voices and when they put Erika on the line I could tell by the tone of her voice that she was really stressing.

"Relax girl, I know you well enough to know that everything will be sorted. I can't believe you've got Natalie hosting tonight's party now that she's visibly showing."

"Pregnant girls still have sex you know... I should know," she answered sullenly.

Touché, I thought, picturing Erika grinning as she said that.

"Anyway think of it as another untapped market, I know of a few friends of mine that couldn't stop masturbating when they were pregnant, something to do with the hormones. One of them even went to the doctor and he said it was perfectly natural so maybe we should be targeting pregnant women to buy our stuff, you never know, Natalie our beautiful pregnant hostess could possibly capture that niche market," she laughed wickedly.

"There I go all corporate business like again. I'm just worried about the new girls, the girl I found seems great, really confident and pretty, she reminds me of you,"

I grinned as I acknowledged Erika's compliment.

"But as for the other two I haven't even met them, Bianca was the one who offered them the job and as much as I love Bianca I know that she knows some really rough characters and not exactly the type of girls we want promoting N&S products."

"I wouldn't worry too much, I'm sure everyone there will either be too distracted by the strippers, the competitions, and of course our fantastic products to even notice the girls," I said reassuringly. "Think yourself lucky that you're over there, over here all I've got is grey and damp drizzle, hospitals, bland English food and misery for company. Is it wrong of me to hope that Sinead's parents decide to pull the plug soon?" I asked.

"God Vanessa, you can't say that," Erika replied, the shock of what I'd said clearly noticeable in her voice.

"I'm sorry Erika, I don't mean it in a bad way, it's just that, well, there's no chance of her coming out of this and all the while her parents are mourning, Antonio is mourning and for what? The only thing keeping the girl alive is some wires and tubes. As harsh as it sounds I really think that these people need to move on, let the girl go in dignity, mourn her passing and get on with their lives. Am I being a bitch by thinking like this?"

"No Vanessa I guess not, I understand what you're saying but it's really the type of thing that you're allowed to think but not really say, like when a fat girl asks you if she looks fat in a particular dress when the truth is she looks fat in everything she wears you don't say to her, yeah love, you look fucking huge."

She started laughing and I laughed too and it felt good to laugh, it felt as though I hadn't laughed for ages and then, suddenly, the realisation that I wanted Sinead dead was what had instigated the laughter caused me to stop laughing in a flash.

"Listen love, I've got to go. Break a leg and have a good time. Ciao to my babies."

"Just hang in there Vanessa and for God's sake keep your thoughts to yourself and let them make their own decisions. God it must be awful to be in their position. Don't worry about anything back here, everything is under control, even Angie. Take care; I'll see you later."

I put down the phone and proceeded to cry hard for the first time since I'd arrived in the UK.

Sinead's dad was one of those hearty, jovial Irish characters with deep laughter lines around his twinkling blue eyes; eyes that I was sure could still charm the knickers off of a nun. Even though he was mourning you could still see the real man through the veil of misery that surrounded him and I couldn't help feeling the deepest sympathy for him, here he was burdened into becoming his only daughter's executioner. I could tell that he was a strong man by the way he carried himself straight and proud as they returned from the ICU, his arm around his wife's waist as if he were keeping her from just collapsing into a blubbering heap. Antonio wasn't crying this time and I put it down to Sinead's dad's pride rubbing off on Antonio. This at least gave me hope that Antonio could be rescued from the shell of a person that he'd become since the accident.

We joined Sinead's parents for a surprisingly lovely lunch at a nearby restaurant that the hotel had recommended and it was just after eating that her dad dropped the bombshell.

"Tonight I'm signing the release document to switch off the machine. We're going to allow them to do it tomorrow morning. Catherine and I have discussed this and we've agreed to allow the doctors to harvest any useable organs..."

His bottom lip began to quiver but he took a deep breath and continued.

"I know that this is what Sinead would have wanted, to help people right up until the very end of her life. Antonio," He glanced over at him and looked him straight in his eye, a sad and sincere man.

"I want to thank you for making Sinead happy over the last few months. I know that it hasn't been easy for you to move over to Ireland to start a new life for yourself and that you only did it because Sinead wanted to return and I know how happy you made my girl so thank you for that. I shall arrange for Sinead's body to be flown over to Ireland as soon as possible where she can be buried on the family plot.

It's a terrible thing to be burying your own child to be sure but it's even worse just letting her waste away on that there machine."

I swallowed hard as he wiped at the corner of his eyes with his fingers.

"I refuse to cry," he said stubbornly. "I'm here to bid farewell to my girl who I love dearly and will forever love until my dying day and I'm hoping that God will forgive me for allowing the doctors to turn off the machine. If I could take her place I would do it in a heartbeat, but I'm a realist and I know that perhaps Sinead's passing will allow somebody else the chance to take her place and perhaps they may get lucky and be the one that recovers. Life can be cruel, but I'm grateful for the time I spent with my daughter and I know that those times will never be forgotten and will remain forever the happiest times of my life."

He paused and raised his glass of fruit juice.

"To Sinead; May she forever live in our hearts."

"To Sinead," we chorused, all of us besides Catherine blinking back tears; hers had already soaked through her napkin.

CHAPTER FIFTY SIX

Sunday was the first time I got to see Sinead since I'd arrived. I hadn't wanted to go in to that cold oppressive room but I felt that it was the right thing to do. All traces of her life support had been removed and she looked similar, if not a little whiter, to the last time I'd seen her back in Fuerteventura. As the sheet had been pulled up just above her waist and her head trauma was on the back of her head there was no real evidence of her damaged body and it seemed surreal that she was actually dead. When my father had died he had pretty much wasted away, reduced to an emaciated and wrinkled shell of himself, making his death seem glaringly obvious whereas Sinead could have, to all intents and purposes, simply been sleeping. I gripped Antonio's cold hand hard and forced myself to be strong as he released my hand and leaned over Sinead, kissing her forehead tenderly.

"Addio amore mio," he whispered in Italian.

"I'll be outside when you're finished love," I said to Antonio giving him some time alone with Sinead.

I marvelled at the strength of Sinead's dad. As soon as we left the hospital he began making arrangements for the transportation of Sinead's body over to Ireland. I tried not to think about how the minute after we'd vacated a team of doctors would have converged into that little peaceful room and carved out all of Sinead's useful bits.

"You will fly over to Ireland to be with me at the funeral won't you?" asked a paler than usual Antonio, the combination of his concoction of pills and the trauma of the day's events culminating to create his almost translucent pallor.

"Of course I will, it'll be great to get out of this hotel as well. Do you want me to check on the Ryanair website and see what I can find?" I asked switching on my laptop without waiting for an answer.

"That'll be grand," he said, the Irish vernacular combined with an Italian accent bringing a smile to my face.

I'd received an e-mail from Erika, someone had videoed last night's proceedings and she urged me to watch it but I knew that it wasn't the time or place for it so I ignored it, promising myself that I would watch it when I could find time. I quickly found us flights for Dublin and booked them for tomorrow afternoon hoping that the sooner we got away from this place where the shadow of Sinead's death loomed larger than life, the better.

CHAPTER FIFTY SEVEN

Ireland seemed to relax Antonio, perhaps it was the familiarity of it or perhaps it was his acceptance that Sinead was gone. I went with him to their apartment to help him box up Sinead's possessions. Sinead's mum had offered to help but Sinead's dad felt that it would be better that Antonio do it himself, as he knew that this would be one of the most difficult and personal things that Antonio would have to face.

Their apartment overlooked the river and was shrouded in an early morning freezing mist when we arrived there.

"Are you sure you want me with you?" I asked him hugging my arms around myself in an attempt to warm up.

"Absolutely sure, I'm worried I'll end up keeping things that'll only make me sad. I need to be brutal. Once everything is cleared and boxed up Sinead's dad will come and collect it all and they can sort out what they want and then give the rest to charity."

The apartment was surprisingly light and airy, exactly the type of place I would have chosen for myself if I was to live here, the muted colours creating a comforting tranquillity in complete contrast to the hustle and bustle of the world outside of their window.

"Have you thought about what you're going to do now?" I asked nervously. It was the first time I'd brought the subject up as I hadn't wanted to add yet another thing to Antonio's worries.

"I've thought about it a lot and I'm still so unsure. My boss has kept my job open here so I could choose to stay in Ireland but I have no one here, no friends, only the people I work with. Sinead was the only friend I wanted or needed. So there's Italy but I left Italy for many reasons. Italy has become a, I don't know how to say it... a stupid place. I have friends with top of the range cars, designer sunglasses and clothes but they have no money. They live with their parents and can't afford to even put petrol in their stupidly expensive cars so when I say to them let's go out on a Friday night they say to me they can't, they have no money but they have their clothes and all that stuff...I don't understand Italians anymore. I can't really think about what I must do with myself right now."

"You can always come back to Fuerteventura you know. You can stay with me, I have a huge house now and we still have two empty bedrooms."

"I don't know chica, Natalie, she doesn't like me very much and you have your own life to live without having to put up with me hanging around."

"It'll be perfect," I said thinking about the video that

Erika sent me and hitting on a great idea. "You know a huge amount more than me about the internet and stuff like that don't you?"

"Well of course. It was my business for many years. Why?"

"I've just come up with a great idea. How good are your video skills?"

"I know a little, I know how to edit and add music and I can do a few trick effects."

"Great, that's all we need to get started. You know we do those sex toy parties,"

He nodded his head, intrigued by the sudden enthusiasm I was displaying.

"Well how about we make promotional videos of our entire range of sex toys? All we need are a couple of models willing to go on camera and with a bit of good editing we could end up becoming the most popular branded adult sex toy vendor in the world, even bigger than Ann Summers and whatever the American equivalent is. You can do all the filming and editing and you can set us up with the biggest and the best website in the world. Just think what a great location Fuerteventura makes for filming or photo shoots for that matter. We'll provide all the equipment and we'll pay you; come on Antonio - it's a deal of a lifetime; Think about it, it's no contest, come over to Fuerteventura to film hot models inserting Nice 'n Sleazy sex toys into their various orifices in exotic locations or sell Russian built farm machinery to hillbilly farmers in Nebraska in cold and dreary Ireland."

Antonio flashed his wicked smile, the smile I'd missed

for so long and my heart skipped a beat.

"I'll think about it okay, now let's get on with this," he answered a happy grin still etched on his face.

Was his shell beginning to crack?

CHAPTER FIFTY EIGHT

It rained on the day of Sinead's funeral just as it seemed to do at every funeral I'd ever attended. I watched from underneath the church's overhanging roof as the guests arrived, the myriad of coloured umbrellas a sharp contrast to the traditional black clothes adorned by the attendees. Once inside the church I was surprised to see a large screen at the front of the pews showing an assortment of Super 8 film footage interspersed with still shots of Sinead's metamorphism from super cute toddler to sullen teenager, to the woman I had known and Antonio had loved. The service itself was surprisingly short and Sinead's parents' eulogy was heart-warming without being sickly sweet.

The wake was to take place at Sinead's parents' house which wasn't too far from the church. Antonio was in attendance in the funeral car and had organised a lift for me to their house with one of his work colleagues, a shy, shaven-headed hulk of Polish descent who didn't really offer much in the way of conversation which suited me fine; I wasn't in the mood for talking.

By the time Antonio and I decided to leave the wake, as is the Irish way it had turned into a full blown party. I could tell that Antonio was uncomfortable with this turn of events and when I finally found Sinead's parents I explained to them that Antonio couldn't really get his head around this tradition, and that we were leaving as it was making him unhappier by the minute. They hugged me tightly and told me to take care of him and I promised I would.

We caught a cab back to the hotel just down the road from where Antonio and Sinead's apartment was located. Antonio had refused to sleep in their old apartment, and when we got in I began searching for a flight back home on the computer. The first flight I could find was on Saturday morning, two days from now and I booked it immediately; it was time for me to return to my loved ones and I hoped that I could be persuasive enough to get Antonio to join me in the near future.

CHAPTER FIFTY NINE

Saying goodbye to Antonio was even harder than I'd anticipated that it would be. I knew it would be difficult for him without me being there as a shoulder to cry on but now he was more or less alone in Ireland and not only was he still in a fragile state, but he was also living under the shadow of an invisible cancer that nobody else knew about besides me. He had a scheduled appointment at the doctors for more tests on the Monday and he assured me that he would let me know the results straight away. I threatened to fly back over and beat him up if he didn't call and the truth was, I was only half joking.

I landed in Fuerteventura at twelve thirty that Saturday afternoon and both of my girls and Erika were waiting for me on the other side of the barrier. Once we got home I dished out the Toblerones´ I'd been lugging halfway around the world to an especially pleased Natalie who had developed a huge craving for chocolate.

I suppose it's better than constant masturbation.

They were all full of questions about England and Ireland but as I explained to them it wasn't a holiday and being back in Fuerteventura was a welcome relief from the depressing gloom of what I'd endured in the UK.

Angie was especially sad about Sinead because, although she hadn't really known her at all, she'd seen her in passing and this made it all the more real for her. She asked lots of questions about dying and hospitals which I did my best to answer, but I knew that my experience of someone dying was completely different to that of Antonio's experience so I couldn't speak for him as such.

"Did you watch our video mum?" Natalie asked, the sides of her mouth smeared in dark chocolate.

"I didn't get time love, but I'll try and watch it tonight or tomorrow night."

"You're going to be shocked when you watch it," Natalie assured me.

"After watching Carmel from Northern Ireland swallow the Big Boy dildo at my last big party I don't think anything will shock me."

Erika just grinned knowingly.

"So I take it that it was a successful night and Bianca's mates' didn't let you down?" I asked Erika.

"They were great, better than any of us even, they were professional strippers and they really got the party swinging, you'll see what I mean when you watch the video. Just be aware that it's a definite triple X rated thing so don't go watching it in public. You know Vanessa we pulled fifteen grand that night. After expenses we made just over eight grand profit. Eight grand profit in one night, just imagine if we could do that once a week and still earn from the internet sales. We'll all be millionaires in a couple of years" she said shaking her head in wonder.

"Oh, now that you mentioned internet sales I've come up with a great idea about how to get our name out there..."

I ran my idea about promotional videos by all three of them, after all Angie was our main internet salesperson and, although she was young, she certainly wasn't naive. They all agreed that it was a fantastic idea. All I had to do now would be to convince Antonio. I'd start on that as soon as he phoned me with his test results on Monday.

I watched the video on the Sunday morning and it was a definite shocker. The male strippers were unlike any I'd seen before, parading around the stage with huge erections which they would stick into any of the audience's eager mouths of which shockingly there were at least fifty volunteers. Their show ended with them ejaculating over Bianca's two friends' naked breasts. The hysterical screams and cheers of the women in the audience completely drowned out the background music and I was amazed that people weren't crushed by the number of women that had surged forward just to touch the strippers' erect cocks.

If I had to be perfectly honest this wasn't really the route I'd wanted Nice 'n Sleazy to go down, imagining ourselves as much more of a corporate adult brand, a slightly raunchier Ann Summers rather than something as pornographic as the video evidence implied but the sales from that night spoke volumes and, like Erika had suggested only last night, if we could get in with the tour operators such as Thompson and Thomas Cook, we could charge entry fees to our shows which would cover the ridiculous thirty percent commission costs that the tour operators demanded and also cover the cost of renting premises in which to host our parties. After all "Sticky Vicky" in Tenerife always drew a huge amount of tourists to her show and all she did really was insert huge objects into her vagina.

I guess I needed to be more open minded.

CHAPTER SIXTY

When Antonio phoned me on Monday night with his results I was so excited that I ran around the house, jumping up and down like a hyperactive child who'd just swallowed a couple of litres of Red Bull. The majority of the cancer cells had reduced in size so much that the doctor was confident that he would be one hundred percent clear by the middle of December. He'd given him a new batch of tablets to take to boost his appetite and he assured him that the weight that he had lost from the experimental pills was only a temporary thing and that he would return to his normal size in less than three weeks with the new pills. He'd also received a call from the insurance company where Sinead and himself had brokered a life insurance policy and they had informed him that he would be entitled to receive a payment of five hundred thousand euros by the end of the week. He'd made arrangements for one hundred thousand to be donated to the Cancer Research charity, another one hundred thousand to be given to Sinead's parents to cover some of the hidden medical costs and the funeral costs and the remaining three hundred thousand he planned to keep for himself.

"I feel guilty taking the money," he told me.

"But Antonio, you've paid your insurance premiums; this is what you pay them for."

"I know Vanessa but it's just so much money and you know, if I could give the money back and have Sinead back then I would do that without a single regret. If I'm careful with the cash I might never have to work again in my life and that makes me feel guilty."

"Please don't feel guilty, everybody knows that you would rather have Sinead than the money and don't even think about not working ever again. We need you over here to be our internet guru slash cameraman slash video editor slash promo man. I've already discussed it with Erika and the girls and they all think it's a great idea. If you're not happy staying with us you can always get your own place but really I would love it if you stayed with us."

I could almost hear the cogs turning in his head as I waited for his response on the other end of the line.

"I'll tell you what I'll do chica. Once I've sorted out the paperwork for the insurance company and changed all of our joint bank accounts and things like that I'll come over for a holiday. When I'm there we can see how everybody gets on with me and also we can work out if I'm going to be good enough to actually achieve what I think is a very ambitious goal; world domination." He started laughing.

"At the end of the day my old job was an internet

provider and I'm not claiming to be some sort of expert; how's that sound?"

"Deal," I answered knowing that once I'd got him over here I wasn't going to let him go away ever again.

I spent the rest of the day in a great mood and when Erika and Natalie returned from her scan I was thrilled with the photos of what we now knew was going to be a daughter. Strangely enough it was only when I was looking at the photographs that it hit me that I was going to be a grandmother.

A grandmother at thirty eight; who'd have thought it?

As they were leaving the hospital Natalie had picked up a copy of the free paper which I quickly flipped through to make sure that our advert was in its correct place. As I put it down I saw the headline Sleazy but Nice and I quickly snatched it up once again.

My God we're in the headlines.

There was a three page spread dedicated to Nice ′n Sleazy outlining the huge party that had taken place at The Reflex. There was a photo of Natalie and Erika in their matching uniforms and photos of the male strippers with their genitalia thankfully pixelated. Although the journalistic skills of the free papers writer left a lot to be desired the crux of the piece was that every woman in Fuerteventura should attend a Nice ′n Sleazy party at least once in their life before they die. We couldn't ask for better praise than that!

I found the three girls sitting in the shade of the veranda next to the swimming pool.

"You have to check this out," I said excitedly as the girls

crowded around the open paper.

Fame at last!

About an hour after I'd read the article I received a phone call from the managing director of one of the big hotel chains asking if we would be willing to host a large party for their female guests.

"How many people are you talking?" I asked thinking that it would be an easy gig and that just Erika, Bianca and I would be able to handle it.

"Around six hundred," the manager said. "Will this be a problem?"

"No sir, no problem at all," I said taking a deep breath and forcing myself to relax.

"We offer a flat rate of five hundred Euros and normally we charge a ten percent commission on any merchandise sold on site but due to the nature of the merchandise on sale the hotel has agreed to waiver this commission as we have no wish to be associated with your products, which means that all proceeds from any on-site sales that you make will be yours. I need you to understand madam that this isn't usually the type of entertainment that we would choose to provide our guests with, but the demand for one of your parties from not only guests but staff alike on the entertainment manager has been so phenomenally large that we are no longer able to ignore their demands," he said in undisguised distaste. "I would however appreciate if you could keep it as discreet as possible; we will speak to all the invited guests on a one to one basis to try keep it under wraps as best we can but I'm sure that you are aware of what an impossible task this is but if you could perhaps find it in yourselves to keep it off of the social networks like Facebook or Twitter we would certainly appreciate it." he added stuffily.

"Once again this will not be a problem for us, I can assure you that all of my members of staff are very professional and discretion is a very important part of their jobs. Just one more thing that you haven't clarified yet. What day would you like the event to take place sir?"

"Oh my goodness, sorry I thought I'd already explained when we would like it to take place. We would like the event to take place tomorrow night."

Jesus, tomorrow night...we'll never be ready by then.

"Let me just check my diary," I said, shuffling some papers around that were sat next to the phone.

"No problem, we can squeeze you in for tomorrow night."

Shit, shit, shit, what have I done? The girls are going to kill me.

I arranged a start time of eight o'clock and after hanging up on the self-important man I rounded up the girls.

"Please, please, please don't kill me but I've just arranged a party for tomorrow night here in Caleta." I said pushing my hair back from my face nervously.

"No big deal," said Erika, "I'll get Bianca to do it, she doesn't mind doing them on such short notice.

"Er, we're going to need more than just Bianca to do it, it's for six hundred people."

"Shit," said all three girls in unison.

CHAPTER SIXTY ONE

Considering how frantically we had all been running around the morning of our biggest ever party, the main event went really smoothly and was a much more subdued affair than the party at The Reflex. I put it down to the huge mix of nationalities in attendance which resulted in pockets of Germans, French, Italian, Dutch and Eastern Europeans standing together in clusters rather than everyone just joining in the fun. Sales weren't particularly spectacular either but really this was to be expected as you couldn't imagine these women, who were tourists after all, trying to sneak some of our sex toys through customs in their hand baggage on their way home. Things like flavoured lube and novelty condoms, as well as our lingerie range, did better than usual, but at the end of the day the guests still enjoyed themselves, we still made a healthy profit, all at the hotel's expense I might add, and as long as the guests remembered the name Nice 'n Sleazy then there was always the chance that they may buy something that caught their eye at the party from our website.

The three of us went into town for a meal that night. Angie chose to stay at home to watch some god-awful horror film that the Arabic satellite channels always seemed to be broadcasting. It wasn't long until our conversation turned to the subject of sex.

"Mum, when last did you get laid?" asked Natalie laughing.

"Really Natalie that's not the kind of question that you ask your mother," I answered, feeling myself blushing.

"She's got a point Vanessa; I haven't seen you with a man since we've been living together. I reckon we should go out to one of the popular pick up points after we've finished here and find you someone that you can take home to clear out those cobwebs."

"Come on guys, you know that's not my style."

"Style; you haven't got a style mum. You're still a fit looking woman, you should be pulling loads of guys while you're still single."

"Pulling, ha, I wouldn't know how to pull. I'll leave pulling to the younger girls out there and anyway have you seen most of the guys on this island? I'm quite happy the way things are right now."

"Come on mum don't be so boring. We'll go over to the Rock Café over there once we've got our bill," she said pointing across the road, "and if either Erika or myself find a guy that's on his own that you truthfully can't deny is hot then you have to take him home, that's the deal. It's not like we're asking you to marry him or anything and you don't ever have to see him again but come on, sometimes a one night stand is good for you and as long as you get him to wear a condom, and you know we've got boxes full of them, then it's perfectly safe too."

I could feel butterflies in my stomach just thinking about their proposal and I hadn't even agreed to their stupid plan. I had no idea how to approach a man and besides the one time with Rick I'd never instigated sex, it was always the man that made the first move on me.

I did miss sex though. I missed the taste and texture of a man's cock, the firm suppleness, the way it seemed to have a life of its own, the look in a man's eyes when he first enters me and when I bear down on him, tightening my pelvic muscles, controlling, and then submitting; that sheer sweet abandonment. I couldn't understand how a woman could be a lesbian because I knew that, for me at least, sex between a man and woman had a type of primeval mysticism and a base-like urgency that I didn't believe could be replicated by a women, no matter how many sex aids she used, yet here I was being lectured to about how I needed to have sex, real sex with a man instead of with my vibrator, by a couple of lesbians.

What did they know about sex anyway?

"Okay," I answered, surprising not only myself but Erika and Natalie as well.

"Great, let's do it. You'll thank us in the morning," said Erika.

I led the way over to the bar faking confidence, inside I was a nervous wreck. The interior of the place was just a wall of heat. Music seemed to be coming from every direction and the smell of fresh sweat and perfume was overpowering yet intoxicating. I'd promised myself the other day that I would try and be more open minded and with this in mind I pushed my way through the crowds straight onto the dance floor where I worked up a sweat to match everybody else's inside the bar. During the next song a shifty eyed Moroccan joined me on the dance floor and began rubbing himself against me like one of those tube train perverts that you so often find on the circle line so I returned to the sweating masses below to find Natalie and Erika, who had, by a stroke of luck, managed to find a table at the far end of the bar.

"Nice moves mum," Natalie shouted over the music.

I realised that Natalie hadn't really seen me dancing much.

"Did you see that dodgy guy rubbing against me?" I asked.

"Yeah, they do it all the time here, hoping to pick up desperate tourists. Most of the Moroccan's usually go for the fat girls though; they seem to have a thing for them. If he tries it again tell him to fuck off and if that doesn't work I know Carlos the bouncer here and he'll chuck him out."

"So have you seen anyone you fancy yet?" asked Erika handing me a shot.

We raised our glasses and downed the surprisingly sweet liquor. Natalie sipped at her fruit juice.

"I haven't been looking," I lied. "I thought that you guys were going to point out the love of my life to me. That shot was nice - what was it?"

"Vodka something or other, I'll get us some more if you

want."

I pulled a fifty Euro note out of my purse and handed it to Erika.

"Get me another four of them and four for yourself if you want; if I'm going to do this then I at least want to be able to use the excuse that I was pissed." I said laughing.

Picking someone up in a bar turned out to be far easier than I'd ever anticipated and rather than take him back to our house where I knew that all three girls would be listening in like amateur spies with empty glasses held to the wall, I chose to go back with him to his hotel room which was only around the corner from the bar. Before I left I headed over to the ladies loo and bought a pack of rainbow condoms.

Surely these were manufactured purely for homosexuals.

What I liked about Adam was the fact that he appeared more nervous than I was. Rather than nervous I actually felt cheap and I had to fight the urge to tell him that this had all been a huge mistake before I turned tail and fled, but he was a lovely kisser and I think that it was only this that stopped my inexplicable urge to run.

His room was small and had little else but a bed and a cupboard which meant there was nothing to distract us from what was about to happen. I took the lead and began undressing, my fingers fumbling with my buttons like a nervous teenager.

"Should I turn off the light?" he asked as he began undressing.

Leaning over I switched on the bedside table lamp and

asked him to switch off the bright overhead light. I wanted to at least be able to see what I was doing.

I stepped into him and kissed him again. He tasted of brandy and cigarettes, quite a pleasant mix, and he had that masculine musky smell that I recognised straight away and knew that it was this particular smell that had been one of the magic components I'd been missing all along. I ran my hand across his firm naked chest, my nails raking at his nipple and I felt him shiver under my touch as I slowly lowered my hand down towards his zipper.

"Do you have condoms?" he asked.

"Mmmm, I do," I whispered slowly encircling my fingers around the tip of his erection.

I hear him issue a soft gasp as I grasped his hand and pushed it towards my sex, pushing myself against the heel of his hand, his fingers responding eagerly, seeking out my soft folds. I felt him insert first one and then another finger inside me before I pulled away from him and moved over to the bed. I was feeling slightly drunk as I lay on my back with my legs apart as Adam fiddled with the condom wrapper. It was strange to think that I was thirty eight years old and I'd never had sex with a guy using a condom before. I smiled as Adam unrolled the gaudily striped sheath; it looked like a stick of rock, over his engorged member. I wondered if it would feel any different to what I was used to but I can happily report that it didn't and, as he eased himself into me, I felt an immense sense of relief that I had finally shaken off my irrational fear of the dreaded one night stand. Okay I admit it wasn't the first time I'd had a one night stand but the night I'd spent with Roger was different insofar as I hadn't gone out of my way to pick him up, and when it had happened it had felt as though we'd been on a date beforehand and somehow that had made it feel like a natural procession. This on the other hand was exactly what it was; we were both just using each other for sex. We hadn't been on a date, we hardly knew each other and neither of us had plans to see each other ever again. I'm not sure, but I think Adam said he was flying back home tomorrow and that was the point, it wasn't important.

Sometimes a girl just wants to be fucked; is that so bad?

I had to knock on the taxi driver's window to stir him from his slumber in order to get a cab home. It was five thirty in the morning and was still dark. I'd left Adam fast asleep and snoring on his back. I knew I'd given him a going away present that he'd never forget.

When I inserted my key into the lock as silently as I could Erika was sat up waiting for me.

"So how was it?" she asked grinning bravely. You could see the relief that I was home clearly written on her face.

"Good, no it was great actually."

"And how do you feel?"

"Well by the third time I was getting a little sore,"

"No, no that's not what I mean, I mean you don't feel bad or anything do you? To be honest we both felt quite guilty into forcing you into doing what you did by the time we got home."

"Erika, one thing you have to understand about me is if I don't want to do something then I won't. Nobody forced me to go with Adam tonight, I did it because I wanted to, no regrets, no remorse or anything like that."

"Good, good. I couldn't sleep for worrying about you; three times hey, you'll be needing some cranberry juice for the next few days I guess. You want a cup of tea or something?"

"No love, I'm going to hit the shower then it's bedtime for me."

"Yeah clear off and get in that shower, I can smell the sex on you from here," she said laughing.

I slept until ten thirty when I was roused by Natalie bringing me a cup of tea and a couple of slices of toast.

"You okay?" she asked nervously.

She reached out and pushed the hair from my face, kissing me lightly on the forehead.

"I'm sorry mum, we shouldn't have backed you in a corner like that."

"There's nothing to be sorry about love: I quite enjoyed it truth be told," I said propping myself up on my pillow.

Natalie smiled, the look of relief on her face, like Erika's earlier, plainly obvious.

"Oh Antonio phoned earlier, he told me not to wake you but he's booked a flight over for next week Tuesday and he's going to be staying with us until he decides what to do."

"Tuesday, this Tuesday?" I asked still not properly awake.

"No mum, the Tuesday after this one."

I couldn't wait to see him again.

CHAPTER SIXTY TWO

I counted down the days until Tuesday arrived and I was like a giddy schoolgirl as I waited for his flight to come in. I felt as though Antonio and I had been through so many hardships together that we were like an old married couple that had been separated somewhere along the way by forces beyond our control.

I hadn't told Erika or Natalie but all the while whilst I was having sex with Adam all I was thinking about was Antonio. It wasn't as though Antonio was the world's greatest lover or anything like that but we shared a closeness that I hadn't yet experienced with any other man; I wondered if he felt the same way about me.

When he stepped through the arrival gates he still looked painfully thin but less gaunt than when I'd last seen him. He flashed his wicked smile and I knew then that he was getting back to his old self.

"Vanessa, you're looking better every time I see you,"

he said, hugging me fiercely before planting the two traditional Spanish kisses on my cheeks.

I thought back to the first time he'd kissed me that way outside of my little apartment when I first arrived on the island; how shocked I had been!

"You're looking better too love; now let's get you outside and get some sun on that milk bottle body of yours. Nobody here will believe that you're Italian."

"Impressive house," said Antonio as I pulled into the drive.

All three girls came over to greet him and he looked slightly overwhelmed surrounded by all of them eager to see him, especially Erika who I could tell had an inkling of how I felt about him. I showed him to his room directly opposite my own room and left him to unpack and settle in.

"Mum he looks ill," whispered Natalie discreetly to me as I returned to the lounge.

"I know love but he's been through a lot and don't forget he's been living in Ireland for a while so he won't have seen the sun since he got there."

"It's not how white he is it's how skinny he is. He used to have quite a hot body on him before but he's all skin and bone now."

You should have seen him just a couple of weeks before, I thought.

I let the subject drop and instead we discussed our strategy for Nice 'n Sleazy world domination. Angie had got it in her head that she wanted to become a model. She showed us a website that was overrun with tattooed and pierced girls called Suicide Girls and explained that this was her ambition; to become a Suicide Girl.

"But Angie you're only sixteen; you're not even supposed to be on this website."

"How does that make sense?" she asked angrily. "I can legally have sex when I'm sixteen but I'm not allowed to be a glamour model until I'm eighteen."

"I don't know love, I don't make the rules. I tell you what we can do though to see if it's for you. Once Antonio has all of his equipment together and is ready to start filming and photographing we can do some test shots of you in some of our lingerie and stuff like that but remember, if we choose to use any of the pictures or video on our website then we'll have to make sure that your face isn't visible or else we can get into a huge amount of trouble and I tell you this for certain, you'll not be posing with any of the sex toys or anything like that, so if you even thought that I might possibly allow you to do such a thing, you can get that idea out of your head right now."

" I can understand why you're planning to do videos and stuff like that to promote the company but I can't get my head around why anybody would want to be a glamour model especially if you're going to be exposing all your bits to the world," said Natalie to Angie. "Just the thought of how many perverts will be jerking off to pictures of you makes me feel queasy, why can't we just advertise in something a little more normal like *Hello!* or *OK* magazine or even those cheap woman's magazines that come out every week, there's hundreds of them in the UK?"

"That's a bloody good idea Natalie," said Erika, "I don't know why we didn't think about it before."

Antonio walked in. "I heard what you said about advertising in magazines in the UK and I'm sorry to, how you say, burst your bubble but have any of you actually looked to see what is the cost?"

"Obviously not," said Natalie, "I just thought about it."

"Well I don't really know what they will be charging but I would guess that if for example you wanted a full page advert you will probably have to pay about twenty thousand pounds. The company I worked for in Ireland used to advertise in a farming magazine in America and one in the UK. Don't forget it is only a specialist magazine and probably has not even a tenth of the number of readers as something like *Hello!* and they were still charging us eight thousand dollars in the US and five thousand pounds in the UK."

"It's not really that bad for a whole year's advertising;" I said thinking that twenty grand a year was a lot of money but with the revenue that it could possibly bring in then it may just be a worthwhile investment.

"No, that's how much it costs a month," said Antonio looking at me like I was crazy. "I would stick to what you wanted to do with the internet. It costs hardly anything and it works well. In a few years there will be no more magazines, everything will be on the internet and if you've managed to build up a really good website by the time that happens you're already ahead on the advertising stakes," Antonio said reaffirming, if anyone was in any doubt, the reason why we needed him on board at N&S.

CHAPTER SIXTY THREE

It was strange at first having a man about the house but it didn't really affect the way we lived our lives. We still walked around in our tee shirts and knickers and suntanned topless by the pool as if it were the most natural thing in the world and boxes of tampons still reigned supreme over magazines on top of all the toilet cisterns. I kind of felt sorry for Antonio living in such a female dominated environment but he seemed to enjoy it more day by day and he even took Angie down south in my little car the other day on a girly shopping expedition. I was surprised but happy how my family had embraced Antonio as if he was just another relative in our unusual extended family.

Antonio had in the meantime, unbeknown to any of us, ordered a brand new van with eight seats and all the bells and whistles. David, an Italian friend of Antonio's, owned a graphics company and they had secretly come up with a complex vehicle graphic design for the van advertising Nice 'n Sleazy. Antonio had risen early on the day of delivery of the van and immediately driven it over to David's for its makeover.

He returned home at five o'clock that evening and as we were all sat around the pool none of us even saw the van when he pulled up. That evening we held a house meeting whilst he was in the shower to ensure that there were no objections to Antonio staying with us on a permanent basis. We all agreed that we couldn't imagine him not being here with us and unanimously voted that not only did he stay, but that we got him to start working on the filming of our advertising spots as soon as possible. We allocated a budget of six thousand euros for camera equipment and the necessary internet space that we would require knowing that it probably wasn't enough money to film a full blown Hollywood production but it was enough for Antonio to begin testing the waters with regards to his filming and editing skills and hopefully was enough money for us to pay the models that we would require for at least a week's worth of filming.

"Perhaps we could use Bianca's mates, the stripper girls we used the other night," I suggested.

"Not possible," said Erika, "They've got contracts in a club in Tenerife for the whole of the winter season. Anyway we'd be better off if we can find someone who lives around here. It would make life far easier and if we do get another of those last minute requests for a huge party then at least they don't have to travel all the way from the south to do it."

"Yeah I guess that makes sense," I agreed.

"Can I help Antonio filming?" asked Angie who ever since he'd taken her on her shopping trip had become very close to him.

"As long as he doesn't mind and as long as you don't get in the way then I don't think it'll be a problem. One thing we still haven't ascertained yet though is whether Antonio still wants to do it. For all we know he could hate living here with us and is looking for the quickest way to get out of here."

"Anyone want a cup of tea?" asked Erika moving towards the kitchen.

"I'll have one," I answered following her into the kitchen.

"So how are you guys getting on?" she asked me.

"We're still the best of friends," I answered honestly, "every so often the ghost of Sinead invades our space but as a whole I think he's moved on now and at least he's eating properly and starting to put some weight back on. Really he looked like something out of Biafra when I first saw him in Ireland."

"And what are the chances of you guys getting back together?" she asked, a twinkle in her eye.

"What makes you think I want to get back together with him?" I asked laughing.

"Come on Vanessa, it's obvious. You need to get out of the friend zone thing you've got going on before it's too late; I've seen it happen to loads of people. I think because of what happened to Sinead he's afraid of hitting on any woman so it's going to have to be you that makes the first move."

"To be honest I don't know if I can. I'm afraid if I hit on him and he blocks my advances we'll destroy what we've got going as friends; also there's the age gap, there's fourteen years between us."

"Yeah and there's a huge age gap between Natalie and I, but we still love each other and she's pregnant as well! Love doesn't play by the rules, you've only got to look at some of the mismatched couples that you see walking around to work that one out. You guys make a great couple and both of your daughters adore Antonio, especially Angie. Really, you've got to get in there while the going's good girl."

Erika poured the water into our cups and busied herself making the tea.

"I'll bear that in mind, first of all we need to see what his future plans are, for all we know he could have decided to book himself a flight tonight and leave."

"But you know he won't Vanessa, he loves you too, he's just waiting for you and you're waiting for him. Man the sexual tension is unbearable; I bet you'll both explode the first time you touch each other."

We headed back into the lounge where Antonio had joined the girls in front of the TV. I could smell the sweetness of the shampoo that he used in his still wet hair.

"We were just discussing earlier whether you had decided to stay with us on a permanent basis," I said to Antonio.

"I know, Angie told me."

I looked over at Angie and she just shrugged.

"And what have you decided?"

"Oh, I'm not sure if I want to stay here with a bunch of, how you say, neurotic, yes, neurotic women."

I felt myself pale in disappointment.

"I'm certain I want to stay with a bunch of neurotic women," he said grinning.

Angie jumped off of the couch and threw her arms around him and we all took turns at hugging him, welcoming him happily.

"Now I have something to show you," he said striding towards the back door and switching on the outside light.

"Your new car!"

The van shone brightly in its pink and black livery, the Nice 'n Sleazy logo in stark chrome dominating the front of the van. The windows were blacked out and once again the chrome lettering of Nice 'n Sleazy dominated both sides of the vehicle.

"You like?" he asked looking at me.

"Oh my God, I love it; the design is fabulous."

He explained how both he and David had spent at least five hours in planning the design but the thing he was most proud of was the high roof.

He disappeared into the kitchen and returned with the small stepladder we used to get into the higher cupboards.

"Climb up there and check out the roof," he ordered placing the ladder besides the van. I climbed up and began laughing. Almost all of our products had been photographed and printed onto the vinyl graphics on the roof. There were dildos, fleshlights, condoms, Chinese balls, anal beads, vibrating tongues, cock rings, ball gags, fluffy handcuffs; literally everything that we sold. The genius of it was that they couldn't be seen from the ground which meant that only people on buses, truck drivers and people in high-rise buildings would be the ones that could actually see them. This would therefore eliminate the chance of people being offended and complaining to the police. Also the bright silver N&S on the roof meant that whoever saw the roof would never forget where they had seen all of our fantastic products.

"We were going to do the van in a flesh colour but we thought that it would look really strange so we chose to go with the pink and black, it's got full air-con, seats eight people and has a roaming onboard wi-fi internet system that I managed to buy from a supplier in Puerto; it's the only one of its kind on the island. The great thing about this van is that it is as comfortable as a car to drive, it has plenty of space to carry all of your products when you pick them up from customs or when you take them to a party and the sound system is brilliant, listen to this,"

He turned on the stereo and everybody began dancing on our driveway. I don't think I'd ever seen him as happy; even when he'd told me that Sinead and him were getting engaged didn't come close and I knew then that Erika was right and that I had to strike while the iron was hot and make my move soon.

CHAPTER SIXTY FOUR

Antonio refused to take any of our money for the camera equipment on condition that we allowed him to build an editing studio in the garage. He didn't require the whole garage so with a bit of shifting boxes around we managed to create a big enough working space for him. Angie was pleased to be sharing the space with Antonio as well so that made things easier. According to statistics our website was receiving around three hundred hits a day and Antonio had set up hundreds of links that helped to make our website appear near the top of the page whenever anyone searched for adult sex toys.

We were playing with the big boys now.

Angie was receiving around ten orders a day which was nowhere near our intended target but was sufficient to bring in a satisfactory income. We noticed that most of the online products that we sold were of the extreme variety and, to be honest, I worried about what it was doing for

Angie's idealism on sex and sexuality, although she seemed rather under whelmed by it all. I did wonder however about what might be going on in her head as she packed up some of our more scary products.

Although it was only the beginning of October we had to start thinking about the Christmas rush. The suppliers had sent us a great Christmas catalogue featuring sexy Santa outfits and many strange and unusual vibrators, I mean Rudolph the Red Nosed Reindeer clit massager; who makes these things and even more disturbing, who actually uses these things? Anyway the fact that they were already planning for Christmas was a good indication that we should be doing the same thing as well which meant we had to buy more stock. We tripled our usual order inventory and hoped we wouldn't end up sitting on hundreds of vibrators, well not figuratively anyway.

Antonio had found a fantastic high definition television quality camera for sale in Gran Canaria the night before on the internet and asked if I'd fly over with him when he picked it up. We planned to make a little holiday of it and had booked two nights in a lovely looking five star hotel near the infamous sand dunes. I'd never been over to Las Palmas and I was looking forward to a little retail therapy as I'd heard that there were some great shoe shops over there.

Once again I left Erika with the girls knowing that they were in safe hands.

"Don't do anything I wouldn't do," she said as we left.

That leaves my options wide open, I though, *I'd seen her rubber cat-suit and gas mask!*

The flight over was a scary bumpy affair which

fortunately didn't take very long. We were no sooner in the air before we were beginning to land. We picked up a bright red Volvo convertible at the airport and threaded our way through the traffic listening to an old eighties compilation CD I'd chucked into my bag.

"I love all this old stuff," said Antonio not realising how much his offhand remark stung. Most of what he called old stuff seemed like only yesterday to me.

"This is a nice car," I said, shifting in the cream leather seat, keen to change the subject.

"It's nice but it has no sat-nav and I'm not really sure where the TV station is. When I get chance I'll pull over and give the guy a ring."

After a quick phone call directions were exchanged and by two o'clock money had changed hands making Antonio an official owner of a really small hand held high quality movie camera. Transactions completed we headed back towards the beachfront area for a late lunch before kicking off our shoes and taking a stroll along the warm sand.

"Should we take a quick dip?" I asked.

"No way Vanessa, the water will be freezing and we haven't got anything to swim in."

"We don't need anything to swim in, we can swim naked."

Antonio looked around at the few people scattered around the beach.

"We can't swim naked; there's people around."

"So what, they don't know you so why should you care? Come on, I dare you." I said lifting my tee shirt over my head and removing my bra.

Antonio watched me, a twinkle of amusement in his eye.

"It's dangerous to swim after eating," he stated, watching me as I twisted my skirt around and began unzipping it, allowing it to pool at my feet in the sand. "What if someone steals our clothes?"

"Then we go back to the hotel naked," I said hooking my thumbs under the elastic of my knickers and dropping them onto my skirt.

Antonio drew in a sharp intake of breath, a familiar sound that I remembered he would make whenever I touched his penis with my tongue and I knew right then that this was the perfect time for me to make my move. I stepped towards him naked and threw my arms around him and as I drew him in close to me I could feel his erection pushing persistently against my stomach. Bringing my face up to his I kissed him lightly, nibbling slightly at his lower lip. He issued a soft moan that I felt vibrating through his lips. I cut it off by driving my tongue into his mouth. I probed his mouth with my tongue as he began to knead my naked buttocks with his strong hands.

The excitement of being nude on a public beach, the slight breeze, Antonio's caressing hands, my hardened nipples pushing against his chest, Antonio's tongue, his mouth, his pulsating erection, the fact that we could be caught in this compromising position at any moment all served to heighten my sensations to a level I'd never experienced before. I could feel my moistness running down the insides of my legs; I wanted him right here, right now.

Pushing my hand between us I drew down his zip and took him in my hand. Antonio panicked and tried to pull away but I drew him closer as I caressed his throbbing member, our mouths still joined and our tongues still probing. Raising myself onto the tips of my toes I pushed his erection slightly downwards and guided it straight into my soft fire centre, feeling my muscles contracting and loosening as his urgent thrusts brought me to an almost instantaneous quivering orgasm. I bit down on his lip hard enough to draw blood and I knew that if he wasn't still holding onto me my legs would have given way, so intense was my climax.

"Fuck," I moaned as I felt Antonio empty himself inside me.

"Aargh," garbled Antonio as he pulled himself from my grip and looking around nervously, zipped himself up.

Erika was right about us exploding once we finally touched.

"Chica, that was so dirty," he purred.

I smiled at him as his chocolate eyes misted with lust stared back at me in an overwhelming awe normally reserved for the giver of miracles or something like that.

"I'm going for that swim now," I said as the remains of our love began running down my legs in a hot sticky trail. "Come and join me."

Throwing off his clothes Antonio chased me down to the water's edge where we both dived in oblivious to the shocking coldness of the water and the startled onlookers. I was still aching inside and I couldn't wait to get back to the hotel to make love properly. After all of my worrying my fears were unfounded. Antonio felt the same way about me as I did him.

This time I would never let him go.

CHAPTER SIXTY FIVE

The two day break in Gran Canaria was, as far as I could recall, the best two days of my life. We shopped, had sex, swam, had sex, ate great food, had sex and then we had even more sex. Antonio had without a doubt improved in the bedroom stakes and I remember back when he was living next door to us with Simone, how much a screamer she was and now I knew the reason why, the things that this man had learnt to do with his tongue was beyond belief. I apologise for saying lesbians didn't know what real sex was like, gosh, if they were as good with their tongues as Antonio was then men would become redundant. Antonio was everything I could ever wish for in a man and I loved the way he would just hold onto me as I glowed in the aftermath of yet another orgasm, as if his life depended on it.

"I love you," I said and for the first time in my life, excluding my children of course, I really meant it.

"I love you too," he whispered as his hand lazily caressed one of my aching nipples.

I hope you love me as much as I love you.

When we returned to Fuerteventura and Antonio moved into my room with me not one of the girls said a word about it but I could tell that they were all pleased for me. They didn't really have a lot of time to think about it either as the demand for parties leading up to the Christmas period were coming thick and fast. We juggled the parties between Erika, Bianca and myself and even Natalie got to do her own baby shower sex toy party – a Nice 'n Sleazy first.

In between ordering stock, organizing parties, booking strippers where necessary and thanks to Antonio, the recent demand for DVD´s of the bigger events we still managed to interview several potential glamour models for the position of temporary, only to be used in emergencies, hosts and for the making of our advertising features. Antonio proved himself to be an expert camera man and his royal-purple haired assistant Angie proved great at getting the models to relax and to look natural on camera.

Both girls that we chose were from the Caleta area, Katie was English and had moved over in the hope of finding work only to end up waitressing for around three euros an hour when the owner could actually be bothered to pay her and she was barely getting by. Isobel, the other girl, was Spanish. Her unemployed parents had returned to the mainland leaving her behind with an alcoholic aunt. I felt kind of bad that both girls could be seen as victims as such but the truth was we were giving them a lot of money to take off their clothes and it wasn't like we were forcing them to do anything that they didn't want to do.

As Antonio's filming skills improved and the adverts became slicker we began placing the thirty second slots before the main feature of the DVD´s that we sold and, just by doing this, we saw a huge increase in the volume of online sales that we were achieving. Not only were we making more money, but the fact that Antonio always chose such fantastic locations for filming led to the head of the tourist board sending us a thank you card for his unprecedented efforts in promoting Fuerteventura as a worldwide holiday destination. I had to laugh; surely filming two hot girls playing with dildos in the sand dunes could hardly be termed an effort for any man but recognition and praise rather than the usual tax increases from any politician had to be worth something in my book.

We had been working so hard and it was beginning to take its toll on all of us, especially Natalie who was due to give birth in mid February. Antonio had seen the cancer specialist over here and he had pronounced him all clear a month and a half earlier than expected. As the girls' didn't know about his illness we celebrated in our own unique way by heading up to the quiet stretch of beach in the sand dunes of Corralejo for a spot of outdoor sex which we'd become addicted to since that day in Gran Canaria.

Although we were still in great demand for Nice ´n Sleazy parties we decided that we were going to close for a week and a bit over the Christmas period and book ourselves a well deserved holiday. Our choice of destination was unanimous; we were going to Mexico, Antonio's fabled land of tequila and beans.

I'd explained to Antonio that the Christmas before this one was without doubt the most miserable Christmas I'd ever experienced and that wherever we went we had to ensure that we were together as a family on Christmas day. I knew that because we were planning on spending Christmas in Mexico I shouldn't expect snow or the same traditional atmosphere that we would experience back in England but it was of no concern to me at all as long as I knew that I would be spending Christmas with the most important people in my life; Natalie, Angie, Erika and Antonio. Rather than a repeat of last year I expected this Christmas to be the exact opposite; the best Christmas of my life.

We left the booking of the tickets and the organising of visas to Antonio as he could navigate the internet far better than any of us and we knew that as an organiser there was no better person. None of us knew much about Mexico, even Antonio's knowledge seemed to come from films and I was willing to bet that most of the films that he'd seen set in Mexico were probably spaghetti westerns that were filmed in his home country, but the truth was we didn't care where we went really, all we wanted was a break from not only working, but from the island as well.

I always found it strange how tourists would gush about how lucky we were to live here. I mean let them try living in a place for any length of time where you can drive an hour either way and fall off of the end. Sometimes you have to escape the rock just to remember that there is actually another world out there.

Once we had taken Natalie over to her obstetrician to confirm that she would be fit to travel at the end of December Antonio booked everything and it was just a case of waiting for the time to come when it was time to leave. I don't think I'd ever looked forward to a holiday as much my whole life.

CHAPTER SIXTY SIX

The twelfth of December was the release date for my book and, although it was always there in the back of my mind, I'd almost forgotten about it in the run up to Christmas. Tessa phoned me two days beforehand to let me know that they'd booked tickets for me to fly over to Las Palmas for the launch as there were no English bookshops in Fuerteventura. I'd already been booked for a party on the day of my book launch and felt bad having to ask Erika to take my place.

"Really Vanessa it's no problem," she said, sighing as she sank into the couch. "Can you believe I've done five parties in a week? I'll be too tired to even pick a vibrator up let alone use one if it carries on like this."

"I'm only away for the day, I don't really know why they want me to bother, I wouldn't have thought that there's a huge book buying population in Gran Canaria. Hopefully I sell loads of books and we can retire from all this," I said, feeling as tired as Erika looked.

"You'll never give this up Vanessa; it's in your blood. You've tasted success and now you want more. It still shocks me how much money we're making. Just think when we first started this we hoped to make enough money to put food on the table and a roof over our heads and now look at us, we've got more money than we know what to do with and absolutely no time to spend any of it. I swear when I get to Mexico I'll probably end up sleeping right through for at least the first three days."

I sank down next to Erika and hugged her tightly.

"What's that for?" she asked.

"Just to say thanks; thanks for being the best friend I ever had and thank you for loving and caring for Natalie the way you do."

I flew out on the morning of the twelfth by myself. Antonio was needed down south to film a party hosted by Bianca and the two models, Katie and Isobel that evening. As I stepped through arrivals with my overnight bag in tow I was greeted by a madly waving Tessa on the other side of the barrier.

"What are you doing here?" I asked as she hugged me like a long lost relative.

"Well, I needed a holiday and your book launch was the perfect excuse for me to come over and the company is paying of course. I only arrived last night and God it's hot compared to back home. Now where can we get a drink darling?"

I'd planned on hiring a car but there was no need as Tessa's expenses card would cover the cost of everything we did whilst we were together. We caught a cab back to the hotel where I was staying for the night to drop off my bag, and then we headed over to the beachfront area. We stopped at the first half decent looking bar that we could find and whist we waited for our drinks she handed me a copy of my book. It was a strange feeling seeing your name in print on the cover of a book. I turned it over in my hands and smiled at the little black and white photo of me on the back. The photographer had done a great job; I looked at least ten years younger.

"So how does it feel to finally have your book in your hand?" asked Tessa.

"I don't know how to put it in words, how pathetic is that, I'm supposed to be a writer, it's weird in the way it feels exactly like I expected it to feel only better. I suppose the best way to describe it would be to say it was like having an orgasm and just as it finishes suddenly having another one for no reason at all."

"That good," said Tessa laughing. "I think editing is the wrong job for me then, I ought to think about becoming a writer."

I spent a great day with Tessa, drinking far too many vodkas and just watching the people as they passed us on the way to the beach.

"British people have no sense of style," stated Tessa, "just look at those two over there, Crocs! They went out with the Spice Girls didn't they? Let's play a game, fifty cent bets on nationality as they pass us."

"You're on," I said knowing that I had the advantage over Tessa as I lived amongst tourists and had first-hand knowledge of their unfashionable traits. It was far too easy for me and just as I'd reached the five euro mark Tessa noticed the time.

"Shit Vanessa it's three o'clock already, it stays light here much later than back home. Your book launch is at five and we still have to get over to the other side of town and get ready," she said gulping down the last of her vodka and summoning the waiter.

"Relax, we'll get there on time and if we're late we're late. What are they going to do; not let us in?"

I realised how quickly I had adapted to the Canarian way of life and wondered if I would ever fit back into the fast paced way of life back in the UK.

When we got to the bookshop at ten to five there was a small queue of people standing in line outside. The agency had done their job well and by promoting me as an ex-pat writer now living in the Canaries, they had drawn a crowd of both men and women who harboured similar ambitions to mine. We stepped out of the cab and I saw the posters for *Principal Prince,* the title of my book, taped to the windows of the bookshop and I felt a swell of pride that I'd finally achieved my lifelong ambition to be a published author.

Pushing our way to the front of the line Tessa tapped her wedding ring on the glass of the closed door and a harried looking woman shiny with sweat rushed forward and opened the door.

"Oh my God, I thought you weren't coming," she said in a thick London accent. "I'm Gloria, pleased to meet you and all that, your desk and your mike's over there," she said pointing to a large desk piled high with copies of my book on both sides. "I've got to love you and leave you; I've got so much to sort out."

Clearly book launches were not an event that happened here very often, if at all, and Gloria had seemed to have got herself into an almost uncontrollable panic. Tessa and I began to giggle and I realised that I was slightly drunk from the afternoon's drinks.

The bookstore was surprisingly modern with refreshing air conditioning and a galley café to the right hand side of the store. A bored looking barista stared out of the window at the crowds outside. I sat at my allocated desk and wondered what the hell I was going to say to the people who had come to see me.

The evening went well, better than I'd expected even if it was dominated by ceaseless questions not so much about my book but about how, if they've written a book, they themselves could get published. I answered their questions as best I could and just as I thought that things were starting to get a little tedious I was surprised by a local newspaper journalist who asked me if I was the owner of a sex toy company in Fuerteventura called Nice ´n Sleazy. I admitted that I was indeed a part owner which in turn led to a slew of questions about the type of products that we sold and a renewed interest in the sales of my book. By the end of the evening I'd managed to sell the entire highly ambitious figure of the one hundred and twenty copies that the store had ordered.

"You kept that one quiet didn't you?" asked Tessa as the last of the crowds left the shop.

"Kept what quiet?" I asked.

"Your internet sex shop thing."

"It's not an internet sex shop thing. It's a sophisticated online store where the discerning woman can choose a reliable partner for life," I said laughing. "Next time you're in the Canaries pop over to Fuerteventura and come to one of our parties. You'll never look at a vibrator in the same light ever again."

"Oh I will, believe me. Congratulations on your sales Vanessa, this was a very good launch result for such a small town. I have high hopes for your book."

Me as well, I thought, *now I'd better get cracking with the second one*

I flew home laden with promotional bookmarks, rolled up posters and three copies of my book, one for each of the girls, I knew that Antonio, for all that he loved me, would not be interested in the plight of the Principal Prince.

On the flight back I began to worry about the second book. I was probably about halfway through but since Antonio and I had got together my life had changed so much for the better that I was worried that I could no longer write about the hardships of being a single woman in a bitter and twisted unloving world. Nowadays I was so happy with my life and I don't think that I would have been able to express the joy I felt when I was together with my family on paper; words just couldn't do it justice. I decided as we touched down on the runway at Fuerteventura that I would scrap my current book and write an epic story about my own life, I mean my life was so exciting nowadays, who wouldn't want to read about it? I already had a title in mind – *Nice 'n Sleazy...* What else?.

CHAPTER SIXTY SEVEN

The day of our holiday had finally arrived and everyone was in great spirits even if we did have a mammoth journey ahead of us. I'd packed very little thinking that I could purchase any clothes, underwear, shoes and things like that cheaply over there. Our flight itinerary read like something out of the lifestyles of the rich and famous. Fuerteventura to London, London to Miami, Miami to Mexico and as a special treat Antonio had booked a flight just for the two of us over to New York for four days as I'd told him on numerous occasions that I would love to see The Big Apple. All of our flights were on economy class besides the long one to Miami which we'd paid the extra to travel business class.

We locked up the house and took our keys over to Clare's, a friend of ours who had volunteered to look after the house while we were away. We were all excited about the journey but the van was remarkably silent as we headed towards the airport as most of us were just too tired to talk. Only Antonio seemed lively as he explained how many time zones we would be crossing.

The flight to London was depressing; *no thank you I do not want to buy a Toblerone, no thank you I haven't owned a teddy bear since I was eight years old, no thank you I don't want to purchase your overpriced earphones, no thank you I don't do scratch cards...*, I thought about writing a big note and hanging it around my neck explaining to the persistent hostesses that I just wanted to sleep until we landed. I couldn't understand how they hoped to endear themselves to their customers by behaving with such ruthless sales techniques, it was like me knocking at someone's door at three in the morning with a handful of vibrators and expecting people to be nice and friendly and to actually buy something from me instead of simply punching me in the face.

We grabbed some lunch at the Pizza Express in Heathrow which even Antonio admitted was good and he firmly believes that nobody besides Italians can make pizza, before we boarded our plane for Miami. The quality of seating was incomparable and I wondered what it would be like to travel in the more expensive first class. I didn't have to wonder for too long for as soon as the hostess saw Natalie's large bump she immediately offered both her and Erika an upgrade to the holy grail of first class.

"Next time I travel with a pillow down the front of my dress," I said to Antonio as the two girls waved their gleeful goodbyes to us.

Angie now had the entire side of the plane to herself

and was fast asleep within ten minutes of us taking off.

"Alone at last," whispered Antonio leaning over to give me a lingering kiss as he slipped his hand under my dress and inside my knickers.

This was going to be an interesting flight.

CHAPTER SIXTY EIGHT

I hated Acapulco the moment I laid eyes on it. If you could have flattened all of the high rise buildings that dominated the entire sea front then perhaps I would have found something that might possibly appeal to me but it was all too brash and bold and far too American for my liking. Antonio felt the same way and after the first day in the sprawling metropolis we hired a taxi for a full day to take us out of the city and into the real Mexico. Our driver Rosa was the only female taxi driver I saw in Mexico the whole time that we were there but she knew her way around and even though her old Volkswagen Beetle had seen better days perhaps twenty years ago it kept on chugging along quite happily.

When Rosa found out we lived in the Canaries she treated us like old friends as her sister lived in Tenerife and in her eyes it was like we were next door neighbours to her. She took us down a sandy path to a little cantina, barely larger than some of the shacks we passed along the way and explained that this place did the best tortillas in Mexico.

We invited her to join us for lunch but she declined choosing to remain within the confines of her trusty Beetle with her packed lunch.

The owner looked like a real Mexican; a real fat Mexican. The minute we sat down he deposited a clear bottle of home-made tequila onto the wooden plank table we were sat at and slammed some glasses down next to it. Antonio lifted the bottle and showed me the worm pickled in the bottom of the bottle. He assured me that he was going to eat the worm before he left.

"Now," said Antonio with a sigh, "this is the real thing."

He looked so content now that he had found the real Mexico, it was almost as if he'd been waiting for this moment his whole life and now here he was, a plate full of spicy beans and enough home-made tequila to flatten a horse.

We pre-booked Rosa for the next two days and she showed us not only the usual touristy things but the other side of Mexico, the decrepit shanty towns populated by some of the friendliest people on earth and on the final day of her being our guide we were invited to her home for a traditional family meal. It was when we arrived at Rosa's house that we realised why it was she drove a taxi in a male dominated society. Her husband had been injured in a mining accident and was now paralysed from the waist down. Rosa was left as the chief breadwinner and not only did she have to support her husband but they had three beautiful children that she had to care for as well.

After a fantastic evening with pleasant company and great food Rosa called for a friend of hers to take us back to the hotel. As a parting gift we'd already got Rosa a Christmas card with one hundred dollars inside the envelope, into which Antonio managed to slip an extra four hundred after seeing how difficult her life was. We told her to only open it once we had left as we knew how humble and proud a person Rosa was and that she would have flatly refused the money.

It was now only two days until Christmas and we spent some time with the girls. They loved Acapulco and had no urge to see how the peasants lived in the countryside. After a pretty successful day of retail therapy we all returned to the hotel exhausted and I immediately fell into a deep sleep. When I awoke Antonio was nowhere to be seen and after a futile search of the balcony and the bathroom I finally found a note on his side of the bed on top of the pillow. How I'd missed it I'll never know.

Gone to see a man about a dog – Be back soon. Love you XXX

He loved using the old fashioned *man about a dog* thing ever since I'd first told him about how my dad used to say it when he didn't want us to know what we were doing and he tried to use it at any available opportunity. I smiled and wondered what he was up to.

Probably ordering more beans.

When he returned half an hour later he refused to tell me where he'd been but he seemed very happy.

On Christmas morning I awoke with butterflies in my stomach. I loved the excitement of Christmas and the urge to run around shouting out Happy Christmas and handing out presents was almost overwhelming but I restrained myself and sticking my head under the duvet I took Antonio gently into my mouth, waking him with a slow and sloppy blow job.

"Happy Christmas baby," I said swallowing instead of spitting; *it was Christmas Day after all.*

"Happy Christmas muchacha," he said. "If this is how I get woken up on Christmas then I wish it was Christmas every day." He flashed his wicked smile as I returned to the top of the bed.

I sprang to my feet and opening the cupboard I handed Antonio his present.

"It's not much but I hope you like it," I said as I watched him tearing at the wrapper.

It was difficult to think of anything to buy Antonio. He had almost everything he needed and what he didn't have he had enough money to just go out and buy it. I'd asked Angie what she thought I should do as she was the next closest person to him that I knew but she didn't have a clue either. I decided that the best thing to do would be to buy a very nice photo album and to print off some of the photos that we had of us together and also to introduce some new ones. Nowadays nobody seemed to possess photo albums and it seemed like a thoughtful personal gift to give to someone.

Angie and I poured over the computer printing off the best photos that we could find when Antonio was not around. I also got Angie to shoot some shots of me in some of the Nice 'n Sleazy lingerie, tasteful shots that I wouldn't be embarrassed about a few years down the line and I was surprised at how good a photographer she'd become. She understood all the light settings and other technical things that I didn't have a clue about and the black and white photos that she took of me were fantastic. I found a great gift shop in the capital where I bought a vintage leather bound photo album and set about assembling the album so that the end result was something I would have been proud to show to anybody who cared to look.

Antonio smiled as he turned the pages and did a double take when he came to the lingerie shots.

"Look at you Vanessa, you're so hot. Who took these?" he asked holding the album closer to the bedside light and studying them carefully.

"Thanks babe; Angie took them, she's really good with a camera isn't she?"

"It's because she has such good material to work with," he said. "Thank you for this present. I will treasure it forever."

I waited for my present from Antonio and when it wasn't forthcoming I couldn't contain my disappointment any longer.

"Did you not get me a present?" I asked.

"I did but I can't give it to you now," he said mysteriously. "I'll give it to you later I promise."

We knocked on Natalie and Erika's door and found that Angie was already there sharing a cup of tea with them.

"Merry Christmas," I shouted swapping my presents for theirs before returning to our room for a quick shower and to get ready for our Christmas lunch.

I have to admit that I was a little worried about leaving Antonio to make the plans for our Christmas dinner but when the taxi dropped us off down a little side street outside of a traditional British pub in the heart of Acapulco called The Hare and Hound I knew for certain that he'd got it right. I could hear the Christmas carols from inside the pub as soon as we headed for the door and I was assaulted by an array of Christmas decorations from all angles the minute I walked in. The owners had made a huge effort; I mean they even had fake snow on the carpet. Cheesy I know but it was exactly what I had wanted. We were shown to our table complete with red tablecloths, crackers and cheap paper hats. The turkey, complete with cranberry sauce and all the trimmings, was just fantastic but none of us could get Antonio to try it.

"Why do you want jam with your meat?" he asked us in confusion.

When they brought the flaming Christmas pudding to the table I leant over to Antonio and told him that this was the best Christmas present I'd ever had.

"This is not your Christmas present muchacha," he said standing up and tapping his champagne glass with his fork.

Everybody stopped chatting as Antonio called for their attention.

"As all of you know," he began. "This year has been a very bad one for me. When my fiancé Sinead was injured in an accident and was left in coma that eventually killed her Vanessa here," he said looking at me with undisguised affection, "she helped me through the dark days. What the rest of you don't know is that whilst all of this was happening I had been diagnosed with cancer," you could hear the exclamations of shock when Antonio mentioned the dreaded C word. "Vanessa was the only one who knew that this was happening to me and now that I've been given the all clear from the doctor's I'd like to take this opportunity to say thank you to this most beautiful and remarkable woman for standing by me and encouraging me to get on with my life but most of all I want to thank her for welcoming me to her family and for loving me unconditionally."

He reached into his pocket and withdrew a small box. I could feel my heart hammering against my ribs. He stepped back and stood next to my chair before dropping to one knee.

"Vanessa will you marry me?"

By now the whole of the restaurant was watching the proceedings and all three girls had tears running down their faces. I'd begun crying too; tears of joy that I barely noticed.

"Of course I will," I answered to rapturous cheers and applause, hugs and kisses.

CHAPTER SIXTY NINE

When we said goodbye to the girls to fly out to New York I was still excited that I was to become Mrs. Minnelli.

What a Christmas this had turned out to be!

New York, the Empire State building, The Statue of Liberty, Central Park, Times Square; I couldn't wait.

"I hope it's snowing when we get there," I said realising just how much I'd missed dressing up against the cold.

We landed in Newark and got a yellow cab over the bridge. It wasn't snowing but it had done recently and there were neat piles on either side of the road. Our hotel was situated at the bottom end of Lexington Avenue quite close to Central Park. As soon as we checked in and dropped off our bags we headed over to the park. The snowed over grass and the icy leafless trees created a stark picture postcard effect that I knew for certain would stay with me for years to come.

"God its beautiful here isn't it," I said to Antonio, my

breath steaming in the sub zero air.

"It sure is," replied Antonio in a poor American accent. "It's freezing though, let's keep moving or else I'll turn into a popsicle."

We managed to cram so much into our first day, taking in not only Central Park but the Empire State Building which was closed to one side due to the volume of snow on the viewing deck but was still stunning and then heading over to Times Square for the evening to check out the bright lights. Antonio asked if I'd like to go to one of the numerous shows on Broadway but I knew how much he hated musicals so I chose not to. In every photo we took I had to remove my gloves to show off my ring and as a result my hand had turned a bright pink and I could barely move my fingers but I didn't care, I was engaged to be married to the most charming, most handsome young man I'd ever known; Antonio Minnelli.

For New Year's Eve Antonio had booked a table for us at The Waldorf. As we walked in the man at the door seemed to recognise Antonio and without even taking our coats he ushered us inside and insisted that we follow him. He led us through the dark wood dining room to another room towards the back of the restaurant marked private. I looked at Antonio questioningly but he gave nothing away.

"Your coats please," he asked before opening the panelled sliding door.

Inside sat an elderly couple but the rest of the tables were empty. Antonio was smiling widely and I was absolutely confused as to what was going on. Antonio released my hand and headed towards where the old couple were seated.

"Come Vanessa," he insisted looking behind him at me. "I want to introduce some important people to you."

By now the old couple had stood up and I realised straight away who they were. The old man had the same twinkling eyes and the same wicked smile. These were Antonio's parents.

Although their English was pretty poor and my Italian was appalling after brief introductions we managed to communicate in a mix of English, Spanish and Italian.

"You hid this well from me," I said to Antonio when I managed to get a word in.

"Well you know me, I'm good at organising."

As if to prove his point the doors slid open and in walked Angie, Natalie and Erika. I jumped from my chair and hugged each of them. They were all dressed so smartly, even Angie, and they were a sight to behold.

"What are you guys doing here?" I asked.

"No time for questions," answered Erika. "Come with us."

Taking my arm they ushered me towards a door at the left hand side of the room, which was so well disguised that I wouldn't have known was there if I hadn't been shown it. I looked towards Antonio but he was deep in conversation with his parents and seemed oblivious to the fact that the three girls had even walked in.

By now my confusion had crossed into that threshold whereby I had to keep pinching at myself to make sure that this wasn't simply a dream.

The room in which we found ourselves was tiny with

just enough room for the four of us. One wall was dominated by a floor to ceiling mirror whereas the other two walls were festooned with assorted hangers. It looked like an elongated changing room.

"Okay guys; what's going on?" I asked starting to get annoyed.

"Tonight mum," said Natalie smiling from ear to ear, "you're getting married."

With that she turned towards one of the hangers and began unzipping what looked like a huge dry cleaning bag.

"My God that's beautiful," I said as she removed the diamond encrusted wedding dress from within.

"Come on let's get you dressed mum," said Angie.

By the time the girls had finished dressing me and sorting out my make-up and hair at least half an hour had passed. I was still nervous though but most of all I was happy. I was marrying the man I loved and I would be with the people I loved when I said those all important two words.

When we stepped out of the glorified changing room the private room was nearly full. I recognised Bianca at a table near the front waving madly and I also recognised a few of Antonio's Italian friends. I couldn't see Antonio anywhere and in desperation I asked the girls where he was.

"It's bad luck for him to see the bride before he gets married; he's waiting at the bar through there, we've got to sneak you out of here through here," said Erika pointing to yet another hidden door. It was obvious that they'd rehearsed this whole thing beforehand because unless you knew what to look for you would never find those doors so easily. Just as they pushed me through the door I caught sight of Susan, the girl I used to work with in Corralejo. She waved shyly at me as I disappeared into yet another room.

"Right mum, just wait here," said Natalie as Angie rushed around the corner to where I presumed the bar was situated. She returned not a minute later, breathless and red faced.

"All clear," she said handing each of the girl a small bouquet of purple flowers that matched her hair.

"Let's go." said Erika.

We stepped through the dining room to thunderous applause from the seated diners.

I could feel myself blushing behind the almost transparent veil.

As Natalie slid open the door to the private room I heard the strains of *Here comes the Bride.* Erika hooked her arm into mine and Angie and Natalie took their positions behind us as we walked along the narrow aisle to where Antonio stood in a suit and tie, his wicked grin a permanent feature on his face, as he waited for me.

The ceremony was short and sweet and when we were finally pronounced man and wife I kissed Antonio, my husband, long and deep to the whoops of delight of our closest friends.

"Steady Mrs. Minnelli," he said as we pulled apart. "We'll save that for later."

At the stroke of midnight we wished everybody happy new year and retired to our bridal suite that Antonio had booked for us, having already transferred all of our stuff from out of our other hotel.

Nice 'n Sleazy

Now this is a new year I will never forget.

CHAPTER SEVENTY

On the eighteenth of February at approximately seven fifteen that evening I was holding Natalie's left hand as the midwife insisted she push harder. Erika was clinging to her other hand and looked as if she may faint.

"She's crowning," said a voice from the bottom of the bed.

"Push," we all cried out in unison as Natalie gave one last screaming push before the doctor was left holding my granddaughter up in the air triumphantly as if it was him that had done all the hard work.

"She's beautiful," I cried subconsciously rubbing at my own belly.

Only twenty nine weeks to go 'til it's my turn I thought happily.

THE END

Coming soon from Blackrock Publications

Suburban Twist by S.J. Lewis & A. Walthew

When teenage convent girl Jenna is invited to hip girl Melody's party she gets more than she bargained for when she is brutally raped by Melody's brother Duncan and his best friend John.

The next morning a helpful stranger Sharon finds Jenna wandering aimlessly around the local park, crying and in obvious distress. Needing someone to talk to Jenna recounts the events of the night before to Sharon

When Sharon's plan to catch the rapists red handed results in her kidnapping it sets off a chain of events that spiral out of control, climaxing in a nail biting conclusion.

Will Jenna recover from her ordeal?

Will Sharon escape her captives?

Read Suburban Twist, the forthcoming novel by S.J. Lewis and A. Walthew and discover the dark underbelly of the white South African suburbs in the late 1970's.

If you enjoyed Nice 'n Sleazy – Try this:

Guilty Pleasures by Manuela Cardiga

Gorgeous, narcissistic, self-absorbed Lance Packhard - a sex therapist specializing in helping anorgasmic women – is writing a revolutionary book entitled Sensual Secrets of a Sexual Surrogate.

When a ruthless mother offers him an enormous sum to impregnate her daughter, Millicent Deafly, a debt-ridden Lance hesitantly agrees. Millicent, however, isn't into sex. She's carefree, joyfully voluptuous, and dedicated to her palate. Lance will only get her attention if he dabs soy sause on his pulse points.

To get close to her, a determined Lance takes a job at Millicent's dinner club, Guilty Pleasures, as an assistant to her irascible and eccentric chef, Serge Moreno.

But for Lance, nothing goes according to plan. He is not only failing to seduce Millie, he's falling madly in love with her.

Lance's life becomes next to impossible when his best friend George, gets married and wants to hold the reception at Guilty Pleasures. Will the truth be uncovered?

ABOUT THE AUTHOR

S.J. Lewis was born in West Yorkshire, England and moved to South Africa as a child, returning to the UK for a spell before settling in Caleta de Fuste on the island of Fuerteventura.

Made in the USA
Charleston, SC
07 July 2014